Surprise Partners

GINA WILKINS

First published in Great Britain 2001
Large Print edition 2003
Silhouette Books Limited,
Eton House, 18-24 Paradise Road,
Richmond, Surrey TW9 1SR

ISBN 0 373 04835 1

Set in Times Roman 16½ on 18½ pt.
35-0803-60312

Printed and bound in Great Britain
by Antony Rowe Ltd, Chippenham, Wiltshire

GINA WILKINS

is a bestselling and award-winning author who has written more than fifty books. She credits her successful career in romance to her long, happy marriage and her three 'extraordinary' children.

A lifelong resident of central Arkansas, Ms Wilkins sold her first book in 1987 and has been writing full-time since. She has appeared on several bestseller lists. She is a three-time recipient of the Maggie Award for Excellence, sponsored by Georgia Romance Writers, and has won several awards from the reviewers of *Romantic Times* magazine.

For Courtney,
my own microbiologist.
Thanks for the help.
And for Kerry and David,
who help out in their own ways.

Chapter One

"And so, by using PCR and RFLP DNA methodology, the probability of paternity can be established to greater than 99.9 percent. It's virtually fail proof."

Realizing that Lydia McKinley had paused expectantly after an almost fifteen-minute mini lecture, Scott Pearson nodded somberly, hoping he looked as if he'd been paying close attention to her words. "Fascinating."

She set her coffee cup on the restaurant table and wrinkled her nose, her pretty oval face softening with the expression. "I gave you too much information, didn't I? I'm afraid I have a tendency to answer simple questions in far greater detail than necessary. My sister claims to be afraid to even ask passing questions about my work."

Scott shook his head. "Actually, I've found your discussions of DNA testing both valuable and very interesting. You have a real knack for making a complex subject relatively easy to understand. I bet you're popular with your students."

"Not all of them. There are those who consider me a real terror."

"Probably the ones who want a passing grade for very little effort."

She laughed softly. "Exactly. How did you ever guess?"

He lifted one shoulder in a slight shrug. "You don't strike me as the type to let anyone slide by without demonstrating knowledge of the material."

"'Hardnose McKinley.'" She sighed in rueful resignation. "I've heard it muttered in the hallways, along with a few variations."

"I doubt you let a few whiners bother you that much. You probably concentrate more on the students who really want to learn."

Her rare, full smile brightened her dark blue eyes and reminded Scott that Professor Lydia McKinley was as attractive as she was brilliant—a fact he'd noticed with increasing regularity during the ten months or so he'd known her. They'd met in the parking lot of the apartment complex in which they were neighbors. Lydia had spilled a box of student essays, and Scott had helped her gather them before a threatening rainstorm could ruin them. Upon learning that Lydia was a microbiologist who taught university classes that included discussions of forensic DNA, Scott, an ambitious young attorney in a prestigious Dallas law firm, had asked if she would answer some of his questions about DNA. She had graciously agreed.

Since that meeting, they had gotten together three or four times for impromptu DNA lessons whenever Scott called her with questions. He always insisted on treating her to dinner during their talks since she refused any other form of compensation for her time and expertise. Their relationship was friendly, comfortable and rather impersonal. Their conversations tended to be more scientific than social. The few times Scott had wandered into personal territory, Lydia had quickly guided him back to business.

Usually quite confident around women, Scott sometimes found himself feeling a bit awkward with Lydia. Having spent a lot of time with competent, intelligent women, he wasn't intimidated by her exactly, but he sometimes found himself wondering what she was thinking. She was very good at hiding her feelings behind a pleasantly serene expression.

He really knew very little about her, he mused, studying her across the table as a server set their desserts in front of them. He'd always considered himself pretty good at drawing people out, but Lydia was a definite challenge. He liked her, but he simply didn't know what made her tick. Yet.

She picked up her dessert fork and glanced

at him, catching his eye. "Is something wrong, Scott? You've been a bit distracted this evening."

Smiling apologetically, Scott shook his head. "Sorry. I'm afraid it's been a long day. You mentioned that you have a sister?"

"Yes. Larissa."

"Is she older or younger than you?"

"Two years older." Lydia wrinkled her nose again in a manner that Scott found appealing. "And she never lets me forget it. She's been bossing me around all my life."

He grinned. "Then you should be able to understand why a half-hour telephone conversation with *my* sister was all I needed to top off an already stressful day. She's decided my life needs changing and she's the only one qualified to arrange it."

"Oh, that *does* sound familiar," Lydia agreed with a soft groan. "Larissa's gotten so pushy lately that I've been ducking her calls—which I hate doing because I'm really extremely fond of her."

"Same here. I'm crazy about Heather, but

she's fully earned her nickname of Heather the Hun."

Lydia laughed softly at the nickname. "How much older is she?"

"Four minutes," Scott answered glumly.

Her eyebrows rose. "Twins?"

He nodded.

"Interesting. I wouldn't have thought a twin would consider herself an older sibling, even with a four-minute birth advantage."

"'Advantage' is the right word. Although with Heather's personality, it probably wouldn't have mattered if I'd been the first-born. She'd still want to tell me what to do."

Lydia swallowed a bite of cheesecake and reached for her coffee cup. "Somehow I don't see you as the type to let your sister give you orders."

"I don't," he concurred. "But sometimes I get kind of tired of the battle."

Again, Lydia's sigh sounded empathetic. "It does get tiresome, doesn't it?"

Dipping into his rich chocolate dessert, he nodded, pleased to find someone who understood what he'd been going through lately. "What sort of things does *your* sister nag you about?"

"Larissa and I are very different. She's artistic and creative and flamboyant. Very social. She would like for me to be more like her, I think."

Scott found it hard to imagine quiet, reserved Lydia McKinley having a flamboyant sister. It made him wonder about the rest of her family, if she had any—something else they had never discussed in their business-only conversations. Maybe talking about his own sister would draw her out more about her life.

"Heather is a dynamo," he began. "She sets her sights on something and doesn't give up until she accomplishes whatever she wants to do. It's made her very successful in her advertising career, but sometimes she doesn't know when to stop. My friend Cameron calls her harmlessly terrifying."

"'Harmlessly terrifying.'" Lydia repeated the phrase thoughtfully. "That describes my sister perfectly."

"Heather's getting married in June and she's deliriously happy about it. She's marrying a doctor she met last year—Steve Carter, a nice guy who seems crazy about her in return. Now she's decided that I should be as happy as she is."

"She's trying to fix you up with someone?" Lydia put down her fork and lifted her hands to her temples. "That's *exactly* what Larissa's been up to lately! Every time I hear from her she has someone new she wants me to meet."

"So does Heather. I think she's paraded every unattached woman she's ever met in front of me during the past few months. And she can't stand the women I've dated. I can't seem to convince her that I'm not ready to get seriously involved with anyone right now. I'm working toward a partnership in the law firm, and that means long hours at the office. It doesn't leave me time to do justice to a relationship. I've tried to tell her I have plenty of time to start a family once I've got my career on track, but she thinks just because she's ready to settle down, I should be, too. She's really carrying the twin thing a bit too far."

"My sister's doing the same thing to me. Larissa set up housekeeping a few months ago with a really great guy she says is her 'soul mate.' Now she's looking for mine. I'm half-afraid to even meet her for lunch lately. Two of her invitations have turned out to be ambush blind dates, and the men she's chosen for me have been—well, not what I would have chosen."

"You, too?" Scott rubbed a hand against the back of his neck. "Heather asked me to fix her clogged sink a couple of weeks ago. She 'just happened' to have a friend there when I showed up. I barely made it out still single. I'm surprised they didn't have a minister there to dispense with the formality of courtship."

Lydia laughed. She had a very pretty laugh, Scott noted absently. She didn't use it often enough.

"I think it's all this Valentine's Day foolishness," she murmured, glancing expressively around the restaurant at all the hearts-lace-and-cupids decorations. "I'm hoping Larissa will ease up when this sappy, greeting-card event is behind us."

Struck by the comment, he agreed. "That's probably what's making Heather so determined right now. Everywhere you look, all you see is hearts and flowers and stuff, and it's been that way for weeks. It's no wonder she thinks everyone else should be as obsessed by romance as she is."

Lydia nodded in agreement, making her brown, smoothly bobbed hair sway around her chin. She sipped her coffee, apparently deciding she'd made her point about the contagious pervasiveness of the Valentine's Day fever.

Since the personal conversation had been going so well to that point, fueled by their mutual frustration with their sisters' matchmaking efforts, Scott risked carrying it further. Now was his chance to get to know more about Lydia—just to satisfy his natural curiosity about her, of course, he assured himself. "So you aren't interested in hooking up at the moment, either?"

"If by 'hooking up,' you mean getting seriously involved with someone, the answer is no, not now. I'm working toward my doctorate degree, which I should receive in May. I'm looking for a full professorship for the fall, and I have résumés at universities in several other states. There are several research projects I want to complete during the next few years to keep my career on target. The last couple of men I dated grew very impatient with my focus on my work, but I'm just not interested in changing anything for now."

"Sounds a lot like my career agenda. We really do have a lot in common, don't we?" he asked, reaching out to pat her hand companionably with his.

Looking suddenly flustered, Lydia pulled her hand away and picked up her fork again. "Matchmaking sisters and workaholic tendencies? It's not exactly a lot."

That probably *was* all they had in common, Scott silently conceded. But even those similarities made it easier to consider her a friend, if only on a casual basis.

Apparently deciding they'd shared enough personal information, Lydia turned the conversation back to their usual subject. "Did you have any more questions about the polymerase chain reaction technique?"

"Oh, I'm sure I'll think of several more questions eventually. I just can't come up with any at the moment."

"Feel free to ask any time. And I'll get you a copy of that laboratory contamination article I told you about."

"I'd appreciate it." They had met at the restaurant after work, so Scott walked Lydia to her car when they finished. "Thanks again, Lydia. You answered a lot of questions for me tonight. And thank you for listening to me whine about my sister, as well."

Smiling, she quipped, "For a meal I don't have to cook myself, I'll gladly talk about DNA and matchmaking sisters anytime."

He chuckled and opened her car door for her. "Drive carefully on your way home. I'll be stopping by my office, so I won't be following you."

Clucking her tongue in exaggerated disapproval, Lydia shook a finger at him. "You work too hard. You should listen to your sister and let her introduce you to a nice girl."

Scott laughed and tapped her chin lightly with his knuckles. "With friends like you..."

Looking rather pleased with herself, Lydia climbed into her car. Scott was smiling when he watched her drive away. Interesting woman, he thought.

He was glad they had become friends.

Two days later, Lydia walked slowly into her apartment, her arms loaded with a huge stack of papers she had to read by the next day. It was already past 8:00 p.m., and she hadn't eaten since lunchtime. Too tired to cook, she had stopped at a drive-through restaurant for a grilled chicken salad and a bread stick; the fast-food bag was balanced precariously on top of her pile of "homework."

Kicking off her shoes, she deposited her load on the coffee table and decided to change before eating and working. It was going to be a long evening, she thought, moving toward the bedroom. Might as well get comfortable.

The message light blinked on the answering machine connected to her bedroom extension. She pushed the play button, then pulled off her jacket and skirt while the tape rewound.

"Professor McKinley, it's Connie Redman," a woman's voice said from the machine. "I'm calling to remind you of the Women in Science meeting next Tuesday at 7:00 p.m. It should be a really good meeting, so we hope to see you there."

"I'll be there, Connie," Lydia murmured in response to the perky admonition, her own voice muffled by the cotton T-shirt she pulled over her head.

The next message played as she climbed into a pair of comfortably loose drawstring pants. "Lydia, it's George. I hope you haven't forgotten that you agreed to fill in for me at the seminar next week. You'll be speaking from one until three. Let me know if there's anything you need."

"Thank you, George," she said, wrinkling

her nose at his vaguely patronizing tone. "I'm sure I can handle it."

After a pause and a hang-up beep, another voice came through the speaker. "Lyddie?"

Lydia groaned as she bent to pull on thick, fuzzy socks. This voice required no identification.

"You're still not home?" Larissa's tone was heavy with disapproval. "It's after six. Honestly, sis, you have to stop working all the time. The reason I'm calling is that there's going to be a great Valentine's Day party next weekend. It's a dance and silent auction, to raise money for the new neonatal wing at Metro General. I've donated a couple of my paintings, so of course I have to be there. And I would love it if you were there, too. I know this great guy, Gary—he's a new friend of Charlie's. He's really sweet. I think you'd like him. Give me a call if you're interested, okay? Better yet, let's just assume you *are* interested. I'll set everything up and call you back in a little while, okay? It'll be great."

"Don't you dare!" Lydia snapped at the

machine as if her sister could hear. "How many times must I tell you I'm not interested in—" The telephone rang before she could finish the exasperated question. Already certain whom she'd hear on the other end, she snatched up the receiver, hunger and weariness fraying her composure. "Larissa, do not set me up for a blind date, do you understand? I won't go."

"I don't blame you," a man's voice said in response. "That's exactly what I said to *my* sister."

"Scott?" she said after a momentary hesitation in which she placed the voice.

"Yes. I hope you aren't disappointed that it isn't your sister."

"Not at all. I'm not very happy with my sister just now."

"Which brings me to the reason I called you—"

"My sister?"

"No. Mine."

"I don't understand," Lydia said, sinking to sit on the side of her bed.

"I just had another frustrating conversation with Heather. I swear this Valentine's Day fever is warping her mind. She's determined to set me up with a date for a hospital fund-raiser she and her fiancé are attending next weekend."

"Is it a dance and silent auction for the new neonatal wing, by any chance?"

"Yes, that's the one. Are you going?"

"A couple of my sister's paintings are being auctioned. She wants me to be there—and she just happens to know a great guy to escort me," she added with a scowl.

"From what you said when you answered the phone, I assume you're planning to decline?"

Forgetting for the moment that he couldn't see her, she nodded. "I have no interest in going to a party with a man my sister has chosen for me."

"And I'm not interested in spending an evening with one of Heather's overeager friends."

She thought *that* problem was easy enough to solve. "So tell her no."

"I have. She's determined. She knows I'm sort of committed to attending—I have a lot of friends in the medical community. She's threatened to tell every unattached woman there that I'm available—and looking for a mate."

Lydia smiled ruefully. "She really *is* terrifying, isn't she?"

"She's impossible."

"So why don't you take a date of your own choice to the event?" she asked simply.

"That's exactly what I have in mind. How would you like to go to the charity thing with me, Lydia?"

She blinked, certain she must have misunderstood him. "I'm sorry, but did you just ask *me* to go with you?"

"Yes. It's the perfect solution. We're friends who aren't interested in anything more at the moment. Going together will be pleasant, uncomplicated—and it will get our sisters off our backs."

It didn't sound at all like the perfect solution to her. She and Scott were hardly friends—

more like friendly acquaintances. They didn't actually know each other very well. "I don't know, Scott...."

"Think about it. Is Larissa going to give up without a fight?"

Her mouth twisted. "I'm not actually expecting a fight. But she *will* argue."

"And when she doesn't get her way, will she sigh and pout and make you feel guilty for not appreciating her sincere concern for you?"

Lydia couldn't help laughing a little at his uncannily accurate prediction. "Something like that."

"So wouldn't it be easier to go with me than to argue with her about the blind date she wants to arrange for you?"

"I wasn't planning to go at all." She ran a hand through her hair. "I'm really not very good at parties, Scott. Like most scientists, I'm more comfortable with a laboratory beaker than a champagne glass in my hand."

"And I'd rather be addressing a jury than making small talk with strangers. But since I have to go anyway, I would enjoy spending the evening with you."

It wasn't the most flattering invitation she had ever received—but it was among the most honest. Lydia found that vaguely refreshing. "I'm not a very good dancer," she warned him.

"We'll try not to injure each other."

"And you'll cover for me if I get all awkward and tongue-tied in front of your friends?"

"Gladly—if you'll protect me from your scary sister."

She laughed again. "She isn't really scary. Just...obstinate."

"So you'll go?"

She imagined the satisfaction she would feel upon telling Larissa that she already had an escort for the event. The image gave her the nerve to blurt out, "Yes. I believe I will."

"Thanks, Lydia. For the first time, I can actually look forward to this thing."

She wouldn't go quite that far, but she would much rather spend the evening with

Scott, a man she already knew and liked, than with Larissa's fix-up, whoever he was.

Lydia sat for a while on the side of the bed after hanging up the phone, thinking about what she'd just done. It seemed that she had a date, of sorts, with Scott Pearson. She couldn't say the possibility had never occurred to her during the past few months, but she hadn't really expected it to happen.

It wasn't that she didn't find Scott attractive. What woman wouldn't? He was good-looking, charming, personable, impeccably mannered. He could have stepped straight out of the pages of the romance novels she enjoyed reading for relaxation after long, hard days in the lab and classroom—and she had pictured him more than once lately as the hero of those stories, with herself as the heroine. But she had considered that a harmless fantasy with little chance of becoming reality since he'd given her no reason to believe he was interested in anything more than her passing knowledge of forensic DNA.

He'd flirted some, but not seriously, making

her think it was more habit than intent on his part. She'd even felt comfortable flirting back a little although she'd never been very good at that particular art. Yet this was the first time he had asked her for a real date, even as casually worded as this invitation had been.

Though she wasn't the type to weave romantic fantasies for herself, she knew she'd better be very careful when it came to Scott Pearson. She hadn't had enough experience with men like him. She simply didn't have time, not even for a man as intriguing as Scott Pearson.

"So who is this guy? Why haven't you mentioned him before?"

Lydia examined a long silver dress on a hanger, then shook her head and moved to the next selection in the boutique she and her sister were visiting. "I told you, Larissa. His name is Scott Pearson and he's an attorney who lives in my apartment building. I haven't known him very long, so there really hasn't been anything to mention."

"An attorney?" Larissa uttered the word with a curled lip.

"I know you don't care for the profession, but Scott's a very nice man. He seems quite reputable."

"How old is he?"

A bit surprised by the question, Lydia looked away from the dress racks to glance at her sister. "I don't know. I haven't asked him. About my age, I guess. Why?"

"I just want to know more about him. You're being very mysterious."

"You'll meet him for yourself Saturday evening. I'm really not trying to be mysterious. I just don't know what else to tell you about him."

"Well, at least tell me if he's good-looking."

Lydia pictured Scott very clearly—his dark auburn hair, glittering green eyes, the long, disarming slash of dimple in his left cheek when he gave her one of his slow, sexy smiles. "Yes," she said, keeping her voice casual. "He's very nice-looking."

Larissa apparently read more into Lydia's tone than she had intended. "Really?" Her expression turned speculative.

"I just need something appropriate to wear for the occasion," Lydia said repressively. "I'm not trying to impress Scott particularly."

Larissa held up a scrap of iridescent red fabric that would cover very little more than the law required. "Why don't you try this on?"

"You must be joking."

"You could at least try it on. I bet it would look fabulous on you."

"I don't think so." Lydia held up a classically tailored black sheath. "This one's nice."

Larissa curled her lip. "Bo-o-oring."

Sighing, Lydia shook her head. "What made me think I should accompany you on a shopping trip? We never agree on clothing."

As an example, she compared the outfits they had chosen for this shopping excursion. Lydia wore a navy blazer with a white shirt and khaki slacks. Larissa's clothes were trendy, eccentric, brilliantly colorful, clashing cheerfully with her below-shoulder-length cascade of henna-red curls. Lydia knew her sister would don the revealing red gown in a heartbeat—and would look spectacular in it. She would carry it off with confidence and aplomb—whereas Lydia would be painfully self-conscious in it, trying her best to hide behind the nearest potted plant.

"What about this?" Larissa motioned toward a beaded column dress of rich, deep blue. "It's conservative, but not as dull as the black one."

Tucking a sweep of hair behind her ears, Lydia studied the gown in question. "That one's rather nice."

"Try it on," Larissa urged. "Trust me. Anything's better than that other one."

Lydia sighed and returned the black sheath—which really wasn't all that bad, she thought—to the rack. "All right. I'll try it."

The salesclerk who'd been hovering discreetly nearby smiled and motioned toward the back of the store. "The dressing rooms are right this way."

Ten minutes later, Lydia said through the

louvered dressing-room door, ‘‘No, I don’t think this will do.’’

‘‘Let me see,’’ her sister demanded from the other side.

‘‘It’s too…tight,’’ Lydia fretted, frowning at the mirror. ‘‘And the slit in the skirt is too high. Maybe I should try the black one.’’

‘‘Not until I see that one. Open the door, Lyddie.’’

Still frowning, Lydia opened the door. ‘‘See? It just doesn’t—’’

‘‘It’s perfect,’’ Larissa breathed, clapping her hands in front of her.

‘‘It’s lovely, ma’am,’’ the salesclerk agreed fervently. ‘‘It fits you beautifully.’’

Lydia turned back to the mirror. ‘‘You don’t think it’s too tight?’’

‘‘Lydia, you have a great figure. Stop hiding it. It’s not as if you’re actually showing any skin, except for a little leg when you walk.’’

‘‘It’s a fabric that clings a little,’’ the clerk explained. ‘‘But it’s a wonderful style for you.’’

Lydia wavered in indecision. "You really think so?"

Larissa and the salesclerk agreed in unison. "That lawyer's going to see you in this dress and swallow his briefcase," Larissa added.

Reluctantly taken with that improbable image, Lydia reminded herself that she wasn't particularly trying to make herself attractive for Scott. But she supposed it wouldn't hurt to dress up a bit for the event. It wasn't as if she had an opportunity to be glamorous very often. "I'll take it," she said before she could change her mind.

Her sister and the salesclerk both smiled in satisfaction.

Chapter Two

Scott glanced at his watch as he approached Lydia's door. He was pleased to note that he was right on time. He suspected that she was a woman who would appreciate punctuality.

Remembering the way Heather had grilled him when he'd told her he was bringing a date for the evening, he smiled. She'd been openly skeptical that he had chosen someone of whom she would approve. "Promise me you aren't bringing a stripper or a bimbo just to embarrass me," she had demanded.

"Would I do that?" he had asked in exasperation. And then had quickly added, "Don't answer."

He defied her to find anything to criticize about Lydia McKinley. A scientist, a teacher, a doctoral candidate. A capable, intelligent, quietly attractive woman anyone would be proud to call a friend. Heather would probably decide they were perfect for each other and embarrass them both with a bunch of subtle-as-a-sledgehammer hints. But at least she would get off his back about the women she wanted to introduce him to. Maybe he could stop worrying for a while about when she would blindside him with the next fix-up.

Prepared for a pleasant and undemanding evening, he smiled as Lydia's door opened. His smile froze when he saw her.

She looked…stunning. From head to toe. Her upswept brown hair bared the graceful sweep of her neck. A couple of soft tendrils lay against her temples, adding a touch of feminine romanticism to the style. She wore a bit more makeup than usual, highlighting her intriguingly slanted blue eyes and high cheekbones. Her shiny lip gloss made him realize for the first time just how full and sensual her lower lip was.

And the dress…

The way the midnight-blue garment molded to her body made it very difficult for Scott to keep his attention on her face. It wasn't an overtly sexy dress, but the effect was still powerful. Deceptively conservative, the dress clung to her curves and revealed only glimpses of skin through long, nearly sheer sleeves and a slit at one side of the skirt.

He'd always thought that Lydia McKinley had great legs. Now he realized they were spectacular. Her strappy heels made them look even longer and shapelier than he'd noted before.

He cleared his throat. "You look…lovely," he said, aware of what an understatement that was.

"Thank you." It was obvious from the flush of color on her cheeks that Lydia wasn't completely comfortable with the situation. "You look very nice, too."

He gave her a rueful smile. "I'd rather have on jeans and a T-shirt than evening clothes," he confessed.

A little of the tension eased from her face. "And I'd be much more comfortable in my work clothes," she agreed.

He chuckled. "So we'll be uncomfortable together. But we'll look good." He remembered only then that he'd brought something for her. "Happy Valentine's Day," he said, extending the hand that held a bouquet of deep coral roses. He'd chosen the nontraditional color because he decided the gesture would seem less sentimental than the usual red roses, but he'd thought the occasion merited some acknowledgment. No matter how disdainfully she'd spoken of Valentine's Day, he knew most women liked it when men acknowledged the date in some way.

Her eyes widened as she accepted the roses from him. "You certainly didn't have to do this—but they're beautiful." As if she couldn't resist, she buried her nose in them, inhaling deeply. ‘‘I love the scent of roses,’’ she murmured.

For some reason, he found himself forced to clear his throat before he could speak again. ‘‘Maybe you’d like to put them in water before we go?’’

‘‘Yes. Of course. Come in. I’ll be right back.’’

He needed a little distance from her for a few moments, he found himself thinking as he entered her apartment for the first time. He’d become a bit too aware of how gracefully she moved in her clingy gown. How pretty she looked with her cheeks flushed and her eyes shining and her mouth so soft and shiny…

All in all, it was a good thing they had made it clear from the beginning that they were only interested in being friends.

To distract himself from thoughts of how good she looked, he studied her living room, discreetly looking for more clues about what Lydia McKinley was really like. Her furnishings seemed to have been chosen for practicality—solid colors, sturdy fabrics, classic styles. She seemed to have a fondness for brightly patterned tapestry pillows, which brightened the room considerably, as did the boldly original paintings gracing her walls. Her sister's? he wondered, remembering that she'd mentioned Larissa was an artist. If so, Larissa was very good.

Lydia came back in carrying a glass vase in which she had hastily arranged the coral roses. She set it on the coffee table, stepping back to admire the effect for a moment. "They really are lovely, Scott. Thank you."

"You're welcome."

"Would you like a drink or something before we go?"

He shook his head, thinking that if he settled comfortably with her here, he wouldn't want to leave at all. He would much rather spend the evening getting to know pretty Lydia McKinley than mingling with the crowd that would surely be at the charity dance. Especially since they'd made it clear that they could be friends without a lot of complications, he reminded himself. "We'd better be going."

She sighed lightly and reached for her purse. "I suppose you're right. The sooner we leave, the sooner this will be over."

Hardly the most flattering statement he could have heard at the beginning of a date, Scott thought with a slight wince.

Scott hadn't been exaggerating when he'd said he had some connections in the medical community, Lydia realized not long after they arrived at the charity event. They could hardly take more than a few steps across the crowded ballroom without being hailed by someone he knew.

Unfailingly courteous, Scott made a point of introducing her to everyone as his friend, Lydia McKinley. He seemed pleased to have her with him, and she found herself rather proud to be at his side. She couldn't help flashing back momentarily to high school.

Scott, she thought, would have belonged to the "cool" crowd at her school. Popular, good-looking, athletic, casually charming. She, on the other hand, had been one of the ‘‘brainy’’ set. Serious, focused, studious, shy. She hadn’t dated much, and she’d gone to the senior prom with a boy from her group who was as socially challenged as she was. It hadn’t been a fun evening.

High school was far behind her, of course, but it seemed that some old images lingered in the back of the mind for a lifetime. She’d been careful since then to spend time with people who were more like herself. Much less stressful in the long run, she had decided.

‘‘Oh, boy,’’ Scott suddenly murmured into her ear. ‘‘Here we go.’’

Confused, she glanced up at him. ‘‘What do you—’’

‘‘Scott! There you are,’’ someone proclaimed before Lydia could complete the question.

It didn’t take a great deal of perceptiveness for Lydia to figure out that this woman was probably Scott’s twin sister, Heather. The family resemblance was strong—same bright green eyes, dark auburn hair and single dimple. ''Yes, here I am, Heather,'' Scott said, undeniable affection softening the wry greeting.

Towing a pleasant-faced man behind her, Heather bustled up to them already talking. ''Isn't this great? The turnout is wonderful, don't you think? Have you had a chance to look at the silent auction items yet? There are some fabulous donations. Steve and I have placed bids on several things, including a really spectacular painting that would look perfect in our living room. You must be Lydia.''

Since the last was added without a pause for breath, it took Lydia a moment to catch up. More accustomed to his sister's rhythm, Scott answered for her. ''Yes, this is Lydia McKinley. Lydia, I'd like you to meet my sister, Heather, and her fiancé, Dr. Steve Carter,'' he added, nodding toward the nice-looking man who'd trailed in Heather's wake.

''It's very nice to meet you both,'' Lydia said, shaking their hands.

''Scott said you're a science professor?'' Heather probed, studying her with an intensity that made Lydia feel like a specimen in one of her own labs.

"An associate professor in the microbiology department," Lydia confirmed.

"Lydia's a doctoral candidate in microbiology," Scott added. "She'll have her Ph.D. this spring."

Wanting to shift the conversation away from herself, Lydia spoke to Heather, wishing even as she did so that she was better at making small talk with new acquaintances. "Scott said you work in advertising?"

"Yes. I'm an account executive for O'Brien, Simmons and Stern. Have you and Scott known each other long?" Heather was obviously more interested in finding out about her brother's companion than talking about herself for the moment.

Scott sighed heavily before Lydia could answer. "Let's go look at the auction offerings, Lydia. That should be more fun than standing here being cross-examined by my nosy sister." Again, there was more affection than irritation in his voice.

Heather frowned at him. ‘‘I wasn’t being rude. I was just curious.’’

‘‘Maybe we should go dance, Heather,’’ her fiancé suggested quickly.

‘‘Okay. I’ll talk to you two later,’’ Heather called over her shoulder as he pulled her away. ‘‘I’d love to have a chance to sit down and get to know you better, Lydia, when we...’’

Steve pulled her into the crowd still talking.

Scott chuckled. ‘‘I’m not sure if that was a promise or a warning.’’

‘‘She seemed very pleasant,’’ Lydia assured him, though she had a funny sense that Heather hadn’t actually approved of her at first impression.

Scott slid an arm casually around her shoulders. ‘‘She’s a nut. I love her, but I’ve got to be honest—she’ll grill you to distraction if you let her. My sister is unabashedly nosy.’’

A bit flustered by the feel of his arm around her, Lydia started to reply, but then paused when she saw Larissa and Charlie making their way toward her. Taking a deep breath, she glanced up at Scott. ‘‘You think *your* sister is scary? Wait until you meet mine,'' she murmured, then turned with a forced smile. ''Hello, Larissa.''

Her dyed-red hair piled in an artfully messy cascade on top of her head, Larissa wore the skimpy crimson dress she had tried to talk Lydia into buying. It fit as revealingly as Lydia had imagined, barely covering Larissa's full breasts, dipping in to show off her small waist, then fitting like a second skin against her slender hips and thighs. The skirt was cut away on the left side to show her leg from hip to ankle. On Larissa, the daring gown looked arty and trendy and chic. On someone else it might have just looked tacky, Lydia mused with a ripple of admiration for her sister's undeniable sense of style.

She would never have had the nerve to wear it in public herself.

Leaning forward to accept her sister's smacking air kiss, Lydia murmured, ''You look fabulous.''

''Thanks. So do you. Have you seen my paintings yet?''

"No, we just arrived. We haven't had a chance to examine everything yet." Lydia smiled at the thin, ponytailed man in a long, straight evening jacket who stood just behind Larissa. "Hello, Charlie."

Her sister's latest conquest smiled broadly, stretching the triangular "soul patch" of sandy whiskers sprouting beneath his lower lip, the only hair he wore on his angular face. "Hey, Prof. How's it going?"

"Fine, thank you." She half turned toward Scott. "Larissa and Charlie, this is my friend, Scott Pearson."

Scott flashed Larissa one of his winning smiles. "I see beauty runs in the McKinley family."

"Oh, that is so corny," Larissa groaned. Then smiled and reached up to pat his dimpled cheek with one scarlet-nailed hand. "Tell me more."

Lydia rolled her eyes.

"Lydia told me a couple of your paintings are on exhibit here tonight for the charity auction."

"Yes. You'll have to tell me what you think of them. But only if what you think is positive. I don't take criticism well."

Scott laughed. "I'll be sure and say only nice things, then. But from the paintings I've seen in Lydia's apartment, I'm sure I'll like them. You're very talented."

"So you've been in Lydia's apartment?" Larissa murmured, looking speculatively from him to her sister.

Lydia frowned at her. "Larissa..."

Larissa only laughed. "C'mon, Charlie, let's go eavesdrop on the people standing around my paintings. And you can beat them up for me if they say anything unpleasant."

"You keep forgetting I'm a pacifist," Charlie complained, then added with a grin, "not to mention a coward."

"You weren't exaggerating, were you?" Scott murmured when Larissa and Charlie moved away.

"About Larissa? No."

"The two of you really are very different."

"Night and day," Lydia agreed. "But

we've always gotten along well enough despite those differences.''

Scott nodded. ''Heather and I do, too, considering. But when we disagree, we do so passionately.''

Amused by the wording, she laughed softly. ''Larissa does *everything* passionately.''

''I'd like to see her paintings.''

''I'm sure we can find them—somewhere,'' she added, looking around the crowded ballroom lined with auction offerings on the outer edges.

He offered his arm. ''Let's snag some champagne and check everything out, shall we?''

The first thing Lydia did when she walked into her apartment much later that evening was kick off her shoes. She wiggled her toes in the plush carpet and gave a sigh of relief. ''Oh, that's *much* better.''

From behind her, Scott gave a low laugh as he carried in a rather large cardboard box. ''I take it your feet were hurting?''

''*You* wobble around in those tight, stiff,

spike-heeled torture devices for six hours and see how *your* feet feel.''

``I'll pass, thanks. A bow tie and cummerbund are bad enough. Where do you want your lamp?''

Reminded of the delicately pretty, Tiffany-style lamp she had purchased at the silent auction, she turned quickly. ``Sorry. I was so anxious to get out of those shoes, I almost forgot about the lamp. Just set it on the table. I'll find a place for it later.''

He deposited the heavy box carefully on the coffee table. ``It's a nice lamp. But heavy.''

``I thought it was lovely. And the money went to a good cause. As did the money you spent for *your* purchase.''

He patted his pocket in satisfaction. ``Playoff tickets? Definitely a good cause for my money.''

``I *meant* the hospital wing is a good cause.''

Chuckling at her stern tone, he nodded. ``That, too. Did you have a good time this evening?''

"Yes, very nice." Surprisingly enough, she had. Scott had been a charming escort. He'd stayed close to her side, had seemed interested in her conversation, had made sure she didn't feel left out when he'd talked to his friends. And he had danced with her, matching his steps to hers so well that her initial awkwardness had quickly eased though her physical awareness of him had been a bit more difficult to ignore.

All in all, it had been the most successful date she'd had in…well, ever.

Good thing they'd made it clear from the beginning that it wasn't going to lead anywhere, she thought, trying not to feel wistful. She wouldn't want to start expecting too much from this man who didn't want a woman to interfere with his climb to a partnership. And she certainly didn't want any man to get in the way of *her* career, she reminded herself. She had learned that lesson very well from a lifetime of her embittered, frustrated mother's warnings.

She pushed a wispy strand of hair away

from her temple and hesitated, wondering what to do now. ''Um...would you like a cup of coffee or something?''

He hesitated a moment, then shook his head with a slight smile. ''No, thanks. I'd better go. It's getting late.''

Lydia walked him to the door. ''Thank you for bringing my lamp up for me.''

''Thank *you* for going with me this evening. I had a very nice time—and I didn't have to worry about Heather trying to match me up with every available woman there tonight.''

The mention of his sister made Lydia frown a bit. Her few encounters with Heather during the party hadn't gone any better than the first. ''I'm not sure your sister liked me very much.''

Scott's eyebrows rose sharply in surprise. ''What makes you think that?''

''Just an impression I got,'' she answered, wishing she'd kept her mouth shut. ''Don't misunderstand me. She was perfectly nice. I just don't think she particularly approved of me as your date.''

He shook his head, looking vaguely disturbed by her comments. ''I'm sure you're wrong.''

Lydia was not at all convinced, but it really didn't matter since this would likely be their only date. ''Probably my imagination. I'm glad you talked me into attending the event tonight, Scott. It's the nicest Valentine's Day I've spent in a long time.''

Ever, really, she thought, though she didn't want to give him the wrong idea by gushing too much. This had been a date of convenience, to keep their sisters at bay. There'd been nothing more to it than that.

''I had a great time, too,'' he assured her. He put his hand on the doorknob. ''We'll have to get together soon to talk about DNA again. I still have a few questions about restriction fragment length polymorphism.''

''It's much easier to just call it RFLP,'' she said with a smile. ''And I'd be happy to answer your questions any time we're both free.''

''I'll give you a call.'' He turned the knob,

then leaned over to brush his lips against her cheek in an apparently impulsive gesture. ‘‘Good night, Lydia.’’

‘‘Um…good night.’’ She was relieved that her voice didn’t squeak.

She locked the door behind him and then sagged against it, lifting her fingertips to her tingling cheek.

Friends, she reminded herself again. That was all either of them wanted to be. Right?

‘‘How long have you been seeing her? Are you serious about her?’’

Still groggy from being awakened early by his sister’s telephone call, Scott ran a hand through his hair and leaned back against his pillows, his bedsheets pooled around his waist. ‘‘You woke me up this early on a weekend morning just to grill me about Lydia?’’

‘‘C’mon, Scott. It’s almost nine o’clock. Just how late do you want to sleep?’’

Thinking of all the nights he’d gotten by lately with little more than a couple hours rest, he sighed. ''It isn't often I get a chance to sleep in.''

''Then I'm sorry I woke you. So, um, is anyone in bed with you?''

''Damn it, Heather, what kind of question is that?''

''A nosy one,'' she admitted.

''No kidding. And—not that it's any of your business—no, there's no one in the bed with me.''

''Good.''

Something in her firm response made him frown. Remembering that Lydia had decided Heather didn't like her, Scott asked, ''Why are you calling to ask so many questions about Lydia? Didn't you like her?''

''I suppose she was nice enough.''

''What's wrong with her?'' he demanded in exasperation with her decidedly tepid endorsement.

''Nothing's wrong with her. I repeat, she seemed nice. Just—''

''Just what?''

''I'm not sure she's right for you. Nothing

personal against her, of course, but the two of you just seem ill-matched. I have a feel for that sort of thing, you know. Some of my friends say I'm almost psychic when it comes to relationship stuff. I know how stubborn you are when it comes to fix-ups, but there's this really great woman I think you should meet. She's funny and sweet and—''

"I don't get it,'' Scott broke in impatiently. "What's wrong with Lydia? I would have thought she'd be exactly the type of woman you would pick for me.''

"Well…no, not really.''

"Why not?''

"You want me to spell it out? To be honest, she reminded me of Paula. I thought she was a bit too cool. Restrained. Our friends know how to cut loose and have fun, and I'm not sure Lydia does. I've always wanted you to find someone who adores you and isn't too reserved to show it.''

Scott thought Heather was being ridiculous. Apparently, she wanted him to be with a woman who was bubbly, demonstrative and worshiped the ground he walked on. His sister didn't want him to find a mate; she wanted him to get an Irish setter. Which would be fine with him, he reminded himself. He wasn't looking for a mate anyway. Hell, he didn't even have time to commit to a pet for now.

"So what do you say, Scott?"

"About what?"

"My friend Julie. Will you let me introduce you to her? I could invite her to the thing at the ranch next week and—"

"No."

"You could at least meet her before you reject her. It's going to be all couples at the ranch—even Cameron said he would probably bring someone. It'll be casual and comfortable and fun—a perfect time for you to spend an evening getting to know Julie. I can—"

"No, Heather. If I choose to bring someone to Shane's gathering next weekend, I'll find my own companion."

"You can be so stubborn," Heather grumbled, a pout in her voice.

"And you are being deliberately irritating.

I've told you I don't want you to play matchmaker for me, and you haven't listened. I'm serious this time, Heather. I'm tired of it. I want it to stop."

"But—"

"No argument," he said flatly, swinging his legs to the side of the bed. "At first it was sort of funny watching you running around in circles trying to find me a girlfriend. I'm used to your occasional harebrained obsessions, but this one's gone far enough. It ends now, okay? No more fix-ups. No more 'accidental' meetings. No more ambushes. No more begging me to go on blind dates with your friends."

"I was only—"

"I know you meant well," he said more gently. "You and Steve are deliriously happy and you want me to share your good fortune. I appreciate it, but I'm perfectly content concentrating on my work right now. You've got a wedding to plan—yours, not mine—and a future to anticipate. Focus on that for now and let me worry about my life, will you?"

"If that's what you want," she muttered.

"Trust me, it is."

"All right. Fine. I won't interfere again."

The promise was made stiffly, letting him know that she was a bit miffed with him. He could deal with that as long as he could be assured that she would stop trying to marry him off.

"So, did you and Steve have a good time last night?" he asked, keeping his tone light and encouraging.

"We had a wonderful time," she answered, still rather subdued.

"Did you get the painting you bid on?"

"Yes, we did." Her usual enthusiasm slowly returning, she added, "It's really gorgeous. It was painted by an artist who uses only her first name—Larissa. I had a chance to speak with her very briefly during the event and she's really interesting. She's—"

"Lydia's sister," Scott inserted. "Larissa McKinley."

There was a brief pause, and then Heather said bluntly, "No way."

"It's true. We spent some time with Larissa and her companion, Charlie."

"Larissa and Lydia are sisters? Biological sisters?"

"As far as I know. Lydia acknowledges that they are very different, but they seem to be close for the most part."

"I never would have guessed. They really are so very different...."

Scott had the impression that Heather was mentally comparing the sisters and finding Lydia lacking. For some reason, that annoyed him. Heather hadn't really given Lydia much of a chance; they'd had the occasion to speak only two or three times during the busy evening. He was sure Heather would like Lydia if she got to know her better.

It only bothered him so badly because it seemed unfair to Lydia for Heather to form such an erroneous snap judgment, he told himself.

He changed the subject before it could get stiff and awkward again, but he continued to be plagued by Heather's attitude about Lydia.

Chapter Three

"Okay, your lawyer was gorgeous," Larissa acknowledged late Saturday afternoon. "But I still think you should meet Charlie's friend, Gary. I really think he's more your type."

Holding the cordless phone on her shoulder while she rummaged in her refrigerator for a snack, Lydia frowned. "Are you saying you didn't like Scott?"

"Oh, I liked him. I'm just not sure he's right for you."

Plucking an apple from the crisper, Lydia closed the refrigerator door and leaned against the counter. "Not that I have plans to run off and marry him or anything, but why do you think he's wrong for me?"

"I don't know, exactly. He's just too... polished. A little too slick and lawyerish. I'm afraid you could be hurt by someone like that, Lyddie."

Lydia sighed. "That's hardly fair. Just because you have a silly bias against attorneys—"

"And politicians, corporate types and stuffy academics," Larissa added without hesitation. "It isn't just lawyers, even though our father should have taught you a lesson about *them.*"

Ignoring the pointed reference to their late lawyer father, Lydia continued, "Scott's really very nice. You shouldn't judge him—or anyone—by his profession. Not everyone can be an artist or poet or musician."

"Charlie's friend isn't any of those things," Larissa was quick to point out. "He owns an alternative bookstore—New Age, occult, that sort of thing. He's very sweet and gentle and deep thinking. Much more your type than that glossy, pretty lawyer."

Lydia set down her apple with enough force to bruise the skin. "You're really being very offensive about Scott."

"Okay, he's terrific. But so's Gary. And I think, in the long run, Gary's more your style."

It was all Lydia could do not to growl. Larissa was actually criticizing Scott because he was too handsome, charming and successful! She was hardly flattered by her sister's doubts that such a man could be genuinely interested in her.

"Don't get me wrong, Lyddie," Larissa said, apparently finally realizing that her sister was annoyed. "As I said, Scott seemed nice enough. He'd probably be just the guy for a woman interested in a hot, brief, teeth-rattling fling. But since that's hardly your sort of thing—"

"Hardly."

"—he's probably wrong for you," Larissa concluded evenly. "Gary, on the other hand, is much more suitable. He's admitted that he's looking for someone to settle down with—"

"Which I'm *not.*"

Continuing to ignore Lydia's interruptions, Larissa went on, "And he shares your passion for classic theater. He never misses a local performance of Shakespeare or any of those old plays you always enjoy."

"So find him someone else who enjoys theater. I have no interest in meeting him."

"Just give him a chance, will you? Charlie and I are thinking about throwing a party to show off our new apartment. It would be a good opportunity for you to meet Gary and—"

"Not interested," Lydia repeated firmly. "I would be delighted to attend your party, of course, but I would like to reserve the right to bring my own escort—or come alone without fear of being harassed by your matchmaking once I get there."

"You'd bring Scott?" Larissa asked in blatant disapproval.

"Maybe. Or someone else I choose to ask." Not that she actually knew anyone else at the moment she'd want to invite to a party, she thought. She had plenty of male friends and knew that there were one or two who would like to spend more time with her, but she just didn't have the time or inclination to get involved in anything right now. She was much too busy with her career pursuits and didn't want to risk sending mixed signals about her feelings.

That was what had been so easy about her date with Scott yesterday, she mused. There'd been no false expectations on either side. She had been free to enjoy his company, admire his undeniable attributes—even indulge in a few harmless daydreams—without worrying that her heart would be broken since she wasn't in danger of creating false hopes.

All in all, he'd been the perfect escort at this point in her life, she decided. She wondered if he would be interested in spending another totally undemanding evening with her. If she could get up the nerve to suggest it to him.

"Fine," Larissa grumbled. "Bring whoever you like. Or come alone. Either way, Gary will be there. You might just discover that I know exactly what you need."

"And *you* might have to admit that I'm the only one who really knows what I need," Lydia retorted.

All she needed, she thought as she hung up the phone a few minutes later, was a friend. And Scott had very generously offered just that.

"You're sure I'm dressed appropriately?" Lydia fretted on the following Saturday afternoon.

Sitting behind the wheel of his little sports car, Scott smiled. "Relax, Lydia. You look great."

She smoothed the khaki slacks she wore with a thin white twin sweater set. "What can I expect to happen at this party?"

He chuckled, amused at her uncharacteristic show of nerves. "I take it you're the type of person who doesn't like surprises?"

"No," she admitted. "I like to have everything planned and spelled out for me in advance. Not knowing what to expect makes me nervous.''

''I hate to tell you this, but you can never know what to expect at one of these parties.''

She groaned softly.

Reaching over to pat her clenched hands, Scott added reassuringly, ''There's really nothing to worry about. My friends enjoy getting together occasionally for an evening of food and games. We used to gather once a month, but we've all gotten so busy lately it's harder to find the time.''

''What kind of games do they play?''

With a perfectly straight face, he replied, ''Strip poker and naked Twister, usually. I hope you aren't modest.''

Out of the corner of his eye, he saw her blink, then frown. ''I was being serious, Scott.''

''What makes you think I wasn't?'' When she only glared at him, he chuckled. ''Okay, sorry. Usually we play trivia games or charades or word games that can be played in teams. The game itself doesn't matter. It's just the chance to get together and have fun."

"I don't know," she murmured. "I'm really not very good at games."

"Lydia, you're going to give yourself an ulcer worrying about everything this way. Chill out."

"I'll try," she promised, pressing a hand to her stomach as if she were already suffering from the condition he'd warned her about.

Scott found her nervousness rather endearing. He thought it was funny that a woman of her impressive reputation was worried about an evening of games with his friends. "Just relax and have a good time. I think you'll like everyone there."

"But will *they* like *me?*"

"How could they not?"

A hint of pink stained her cheeks. "That was very nice. Thank you."

He smiled. "Thank *you* for coming with me this evening."

"It was a fair trade," she reminded him. "I'll keep your sister at bay for you this evening and you've promised to help me fend off Larissa's efforts to fix me up with Charlie's friend, Gary."

"This was a great idea," he said, pleased with himself for coming up with it. When he learned that Lydia's sister was still matchmaking as relentlessly as Heather was, he had proposed a plan he hoped would give them some relief until their sisters had moved on to other projects. He and Lydia would be "standby escorts," he'd suggested. Whenever one of them needed a no-strings, no-pressure date for an event, they could call the other. If they were available, they'd make an effort to go along to distract the matchmakers.

Lydia had been a bit hesitant at first. "I thought we agreed that neither of us really has time for dating anyone right now."

"We won't be dating," he had argued. "Not really. We'll just be keeping each other company at the occasional obligatory social event. I really enjoy your company, Lydia."

"I enjoy yours, too. But—"

"We're friends. I'd much rather spend an

evening with a friend than with a blind date, wouldn't you?"

She had almost shuddered. "I hate blind dates. I've never had one that wasn't a disaster."

"Same here. And every time I ask anyone out lately, it seems like she wants a hell of a lot more than I've got time or energy to offer while I'm pursuing a partnership with my firm. You have your own career goals and you don't want anyone to interfere with them—which I wouldn't. It seems to be the perfect plan—at least until Heather and Larissa realize that they might as well give up."

"And how long do you think that will take?"

"Heather's getting married at the end of June—four months from now. I figure she'll start getting pretty busy with that soon. Too busy to worry about my social life, I hope. As for Larissa—what do *you* think?"

"She has a pretty short attention span," Lydia had admitted. "She'll probably drift on to another scheme within the next few weeks."

"So there you are. We aren't committing to anything long-term or time-consuming. You'll go with me to a couple of things. I'll escort you when you need me. Our sisters will assume we're together and they'll stop trying to arrange dates for us."

"And what if they assume there's more between us than there really is?"

"Who cares? We'll know the truth."

"Well," she had said slowly, "Larissa has been hinting about throwing a housewarming party at her new apartment. She's determined to use the occasion to introduce me to some guy named Gary. If you were there with me, it would be much less awkward."

"I'd be delighted," he had said cheerfully.

So here they were, turning onto the road that ended at the Walker ranch outside of Dallas. Scott was confident that he and Lydia would share a very pleasant evening with his friends. He could really relax tonight, he thought in satisfaction. Unlike a "real" date, Lydia wouldn't expect him to pay more attention to her than to his friends. She wouldn't get her feelings crushed if he talked to someone else for a while. There wouldn't be any awkward, how-will-the-evening-end questions. All he would owe her after the party ended was a reciprocal turn at her sister's affair.

He should have thought of something like this months ago when Heather had first started going overboard with this matchmaking thing. Of course, he hadn't really known Lydia well enough to suggest such a plan then, and he couldn't imagine anyone else he knew being such a good sport about it.

He parked his sports car between Cameron's fancy SUV and Michael Chang's aging pickup. "Looks like everyone's here already. That's Heather's car over there."

"We're late?" Perpetually punctual Lydia seemed disturbed by the possibility.

"We're right on time. Everyone else is early."

She cleared her throat and patted a hand over her sleek brown hair. "Signal me if I do anything stupid."

He laughed. "As if you could."

"Trust me. When it comes to intimate social situations, I am definitely challenged."

He only laughed again and opened his door.

Although there were only three other couples, it seemed to Lydia that the small house was filled with people, all watching her in surreptitious speculation. Apparently, Scott usually attended this sort of gathering without bringing a date. Her presence with him this time—following so closely their appearance at the charity affair last weekend—was obviously arousing his friends' curiosity.

She found herself wondering if this plan Scott had concocted was such a good idea after all.

Because he knew she wouldn't remember everyone she'd met at the charity event, Scott reintroduced her to everyone. He started with their hosts, Shane and Kelly Walker.

"It's very nice to see you again," Lydia assured them politely. "You have a lovely home."

Kelly, a petite strawberry blonde with a gamine haircut and a warm, friendly expression, looked pleased by the compliment. ‘‘Thank you. We didn’t really have a chance to talk at that crowded, noisy thing last weekend. We can get to know each other better this evening.’’

Kelly’s husband, a tanned, blue-eyed cowboy with a smile that had probably broken hearts all over Texas, studied Lydia with open curiosity. ‘‘I understand you’re a science professor?’’

‘‘An associate professor.’’

‘‘She teaches microbiology classes,’’ Scott added.

‘‘And are you involved in research?’’ Shane asked.

‘‘Not as much as I hope to be after I obtain my doctorate this spring.’’

‘‘That explains it, then,’’ Shane drawled, looping an arm around his wife’s shoulders.

Scott eyed his friend suspiciously. ‘‘Explains what?’’

Shane’s grin was definitely wicked. ‘‘I was just wondering how you persuaded such an attractive and intelligent woman to spend a second evening with you. Obviously, she's conducting some sort of scientific research on strange and unusual subjects.''

As Scott muttered something that might have been a mild obscenity, Lydia smiled and shook her head. ''I confine my research to bacteria, viruses and other microorganisms. I leave studies of subjects like Scott to my colleagues in the psychology department.''

Shane and Kelly laughed. Scott turned to Lydia with a look of amused surprise. ''Hey!'' he said. ''Whose side are you on anyway?''

''*Our* side, obviously,'' a man Lydia remembered from the charity event said as he joined them. ''I can tell she's going to fit right in.''

Trying to remember his name, Lydia smiled, pleased that her impulsive jest had proven entertaining.

''Don't you start, Cameron,'' Scott warned. ''If I want insults, I'll depend on my sister. Or my date, apparently,'' he added darkly, giving

Lydia an exaggerated glower that made her laugh.

Maybe the evening wouldn't be so bad after all, she thought.

And then Scott's sister approached and Lydia's smile faded a bit. Even as Heather greeted her quite courteously, Lydia once again had the impression that Heather wasn't enthusiastic about seeing her with Scott. She wished she knew what she'd done to cause Heather to disapprove of her—if it was true.

"Are you people insulting my dear brother?" Heather demanded.

"Of course we are," Cameron replied.

"Great. How can I get in on the fun?" she asked with a grin.

"Why don't you guys come up with some original material while Lydia and I speak to the others?" Scott suggested, taking her arm.

"I'll bring out the snacks," Kelly said, giving her husband a look.

He responded promptly. "I'll help you."

True to his word, Scott guided Lydia around the roomy, wood-paneled den where the other guests were grouped on comfortable furniture. She greeted Heather's fiancé, Dr. Steve Carter, and was relieved that he didn't seem to share Heather's doubts about her. Scott introduced her to Michael and Judy Chang, who seemed like a nice couple. They hadn't attended the charity affair as far as she remembered.

Scott turned then to the golden-haired, blue-eyed man who had approached them earlier—Cameron North, she remembered now. "Cam, you want to introduce your friend?" Scott asked.

Cameron nodded toward the curvaceous, rather bored-looking brunette who hadn't bothered to rise from her chair. "This is Alexis Thorne. Alexis, meet my buddy, Scott Pearson, and his friend, Lydia McKinley."

Something about the way Alexis glanced at Cameron made Lydia suspect that the couple had recently quarreled and she still hadn't gotten over her irritation with him. Alexis murmured a cool acknowledgment of the introduction, then subsided into silence again.

Lydia watched as, from behind Alexis's

back, Cameron rolled his eyes at Scott. Cameron, she thought, was not pleased with his date. Having endured a few awkward evenings with incompatible escorts herself, she was even more determined at this point to resist Larissa's fix-up efforts. Her arrangement with Scott suited her very well for now, no matter how temporary it would turn out to be.

The evening proceeded with a great deal of teasing and conversation. The guests consumed an impressive amount of snacks and soft drinks. Scott, Lydia discovered, had a real passion for chocolate and was not averse to battling for the last piece. And she couldn't help noticing that he rarely lost.

They split into teams for games, and Alexis's visible lack of enthusiasm couldn't dampen the good-naturedly fierce competition among the others. Lydia proved to be a knowledgeable contestant in the trivia game they'd selected. Especially when it came to science and medicine categories, she had almost all the answers.

"Man," Michael groaned, having lost yet

another round to Lydia and Scott, "you guys are stomping us. Lydia's a handy person to have on your team."

Scott grinned and draped an arm around Lydia's shoulders. "I've noticed that. We make pretty good partners."

Vividly aware of that arm around her, Lydia noticed that Heather's smile suddenly looked forced. She wondered if she was only being paranoid, if she was only imagining that Heather disapproved of her. Maybe she should suggest to Scott that he should reassure his sister that there was nothing to worry about. That she and Scott were just friends and nothing else was likely to develop.

Because she didn't want to foster a wrong impression, she reached for her soft drink, subtly dislodging Scott's arm. To her relief, he immediately became involved in a spirited conversation with Shane, giving her enough time to recover her equilibrium. She didn't know why she'd gotten so rattled just because Scott had touched her so easily. Friends touched, she reminded herself, glancing across the room to where Cameron was standing with an arm around Michael's wife, Judy. No one seemed to think a thing about that, she told herself. They'd probably hardly noticed anything between her and Scott.

"So, Lydia," Kelly said, sliding into a seat next to her, "you study germs and bacteria and stuff?"

Smiling, Lydia nodded. "That's all part of the microbiology field."

"So can you tell me about all those antibacterial products on the market now? They sound great, but some doctors seem to think they're terrible."

Okay, Lydia, keep it brief, she warned herself. *Don't overexplain.*

Fifteen minutes later, she was still discussing the growing concern in the scientific community about the indiscriminate use of antibacterial agents and the potential increase of antibiotic-resistant bacteria as a result. "People think coating their hands with antibacterial lotions and gels will keep them from contracting colds or flu, when those illnesses are actually caused by viruses, which are unaffected by antibacterial products," she concluded.

"But what about kitchen counters?" Judy asked, making Lydia suddenly aware that most of the others had gathered around to listen. "Isn't it a good idea to use antibacterial cleaners there?"

"The best household cleaner is ordinary bleach," she answered. "It kills most germs without building resistance in remaining bacteria."

"So plain soap and water works best for hands, and bleach effectively cleans counters and bathroom fixtures," Kelly summarized.

"Exactly. Antibiotics and antibacterial agents are best reserved for a needs-only basis to maintain their effectiveness."

Judy still looked a bit confused. "Then why are more antibacterial products being produced all the time?"

"Because they sell merchandise," Dr. Steve Carter answered simply, approaching the group in time to hear the question. "The manufacturers are playing on the public's fear of germs. And people are confused about what exactly antibiotics are best used for. That's why they pressure doctors to prescribe antibiotics for every little cough and sniffle, even those caused by viruses. Antibiotics used in those cases cause more harm than good, actually, and we're seeing the results in bacterial infections that are not responding to longtime standard antibiotics."

"That's what Lydia was just explaining to us," Kelly told him. "Thanks for clarifying this for me," she added to Lydia. "All the conflicting news stories get confusing sometimes."

Scott crossed the room to lean cozily against the arm of Lydia's chair. "Lydia has a knack for making complicated subjects relatively easy to understand. You should hear her talk about forensic DNA."

Steve smiled. "I would probably find that interesting, myself."

Heather, who'd been notably quiet for the past few minutes, suddenly spoke up. "Did I mention to anyone that Steve and I have been able to book the Elroys for our wedding reception?''

``The Elroys?'' Judy Chang almost squealed the name. ``Oh, they're *wonderful!* But I've heard they're almost impossible to book locally these days because they've become so popular. How did you manage?''

Looking quite pleased with herself, Heather beamed. ``That's a very funny story, actually.''

She launched into a colorfully enthusiastically embellished anecdote that soon had the others laughing. It briefly occurred to Lydia that Heather had deliberately drawn everyone's attention to herself and away from Lydia. But then she told herself it didn't matter—nor was it further evidence that Heather didn't care for her. People didn't go to parties to hear about bacteria and the other things that especially interested *her,* she reminded herself. They wanted to laugh and gossip and have fun, not be lectured to by a microbiology professor.

Cameron, it seemed, was still more interested in microbes than music groups. Discreetly drawing Lydia aside, he asked quietly,

"I know Scott's consulted with you occasionally about forensic DNA. Would you mind if I call you with a question now and then? In my reporting, I sometimes cover crime stories that hinge on DNA and the conflicting 'expert opinions' I hear in the courtroom often need clarifying."

"Conflicting opinions are the only defense against strong DNA evidence." She dug in her purse and drew out a business card with her office number printed on it. On the back, she scribbled her home number. "Feel free to call anytime. I'm always happy to answer questions about my work."

Cameron pocketed the card and gave her a high-voltage smile. "That's very generous of you."

From across the room where he had moved to munch chips and talk to Shane, Scott suddenly reappeared at Lydia's side. He draped an arm around her shoulders and gave Cameron a bland smile. "Trying to make time with my date, Cam?"

Cameron glanced pointedly across the room

to where Alexis looked almost comatose with boredom. "Actually, I'm going to take *my* date home before she completely ruins the evening. She's ticked off at me because I won't go with her to some sort of family reunion next weekend. You know I don't do family things."

"So this is your last date with Alexis?"

Cameron nodded fatalistically. "I believe it is."

Scott's smile had a wicked edge to it. "I'll tell Heather. I'm sure she would be absolutely delighted to fix you up with someone. She says she has a talent for that sort of thing."

Cameron shuddered. "Thanks, but don't bother. I'll find my own companionship when I want it."

Scott looked pointedly at the shirt pocket in which Cameron had slipped Lydia's card. "Is that right?"

Cameron only smiled at Scott before turning to Lydia. "It's been a pleasure talking to you. You'll be hearing from me."

She nodded, well aware that Cameron was much more interested in her education than anything else about her. She wasn't oblivious to the attractions of his bright blue eyes and flashing smile, but there was no real chemistry between them. Maybe they could be friends, she mused. She always welcomed new friends.

Scott's arm tightened a bit around her shoulders. If she didn't know better, she would think his behavior indicated masculine possessiveness. She assumed he was putting on this act to further discourage his sister's matchmaking, but she intended to ask him to stop. She had agreed to keep him company at a couple of social occasions, but she saw no reason to resort to outright deception.

Chapter Four

"Hey, Shane," Michael said after Cameron and Alexis had departed, "did you get that new truck you were looking at?"

Kelly groaned. "Yes, he did. And he's hardly gotten out of it for the past three days."

Shane grinned expectantly. "You guys want to see it? It's a real honey."

Michael, Steve and Scott all jumped at the offer to examine Shane's new wheels. The women chose to remain inside. Inviting them all to sit down and make themselves comfortable in the den, Kelly poured coffee all around.

"Kelly, have you heard from Amber lately?" Heather asked, settling on the couch beside Judy.

From a wing chair that matched the one in which Lydia sat, Kelly nodded. "She called a couple of weeks ago. She loves living in Austin, and she's dating a guy she says is really nice. It sounded like it's getting serious."

"Oh, good. I hope she's happy. She deserves to be."

Kelly glanced toward Lydia, seeming to realize that she was being left out of the conversation about someone she didn't know. "Amber's a friend who moved to Austin last spring. She was a part of our group for years, and it still seems odd at times for her not to be here."

"She made the mistake of getting involved with Cameron," Heather added. "It was a disaster from the beginning, as everyone who knew them realized, but she wouldn't listen when we tried to warn her, and she ended up with a broken heart."

Lydia wondered if Heather was trying to

make a point toward her, then told herself again to stop being paranoid.

"Cameron tried to make it work," Kelly said mildly, sounding as though they'd had this discussion many times before. "He and Amber just didn't want the same things in life."

Heather shrugged. "I knew from the start it was a bad match. I have a sixth sense for that sort of thing, you know. I knew the minute I saw Steve fourteen months ago that he was the man for me."

Judy looked encouragingly at Lydia as if she, too, wanted to make sure Lydia didn't feel left out. "How long have you and Scott known each other, Lydia?"

Aware of Heather watching her, she answered, "We met last year in the parking lot of our apartment complex."

"And have you been dating long?"

Again, Lydia worded her answer carefully. "We've dined together a few times. And we attended the charity thing last weekend, of course."

"We're all very fond of Scott," Kelly commented with a smile. ''My husband has known Scott and Heather since they were fourteen.''

Heather nodded. ''Shane and his father had just moved to Dallas. They moved into the apartment complex where we lived with our mother. Shane, Scott and I became such close friends that our parents made arrangements for us to see each other often, even though Shane went to a different school since he grew up here on the ranch. Cameron and Amber were our schoolmates and met Shane through us. The guys met Michael in college.''

''I was brought in when my best friend—Shane's cousin—and I moved to Dallas a few years ago,'' Kelly added. ''Brynn and I were in a serious car accident the night we arrived in town. Brynn wasn't hurt, but I messed my legs up pretty badly, which left me with a limp—and some very special friends among the kind people who took care of me.''

Lydia had noticed the limp although it was slight. She found it interesting that Kelly seemed to think of the accident in positive rather than negative terms. She was, apparently, the type who looked for the silver lining in every dark cloud—a trait Lydia had always admired.

"Michael and I married four months ago," Judy said proudly. "Now I'm part of the gang, too."

Lydia couldn't help smiling. Even though Judy made it sound as though she had been accepted into an exclusive society of some sort, Lydia suspected that they welcomed newcomers because they were so casual and friendly. They'd been very pleasant to Alexis, for example, even as badly as she had behaved in return.

As for herself, everyone had been extremely nice. Heather had actually been the least friendly, Lydia mused with another glance at Scott's twin. She remembered that Scott had told her Heather never approved of the women he chose to date. Was she threatened by outsiders in her brother's life? Did she fear losing his affections?

Lydia would have thought Heather's upcoming wedding would reduce any separation anxiety she felt regarding her brother, but apparently it hadn't, judging from the suspicious looks Heather kept sending her way.

All talking at once, the men rejoined them then. "It's a cool truck," Michael said, unabashedly envious. "Just what I've been wanting for myself."

"Not in the budget this year," Judy said firmly. "Maybe next year."

Michael sighed deeply. "Judy and I decided that she would handle our finances since she's better with money than I am. She takes that responsibility *very* seriously."

Everyone else laughed at his wistful expression, followed by general teasing about his former play-now-pay-later philosophy.

"We have a long drive home," Scott murmured into Lydia's ear a few minutes later. "Ready to get on the road?"

"Yes." As pleasant as his friends were, Lydia still felt very much the outsider, as if she was there under false pretenses. She wasn't sure she would accompany him again to one of these intimate gatherings. She was much more comfortable having him all to herself—to discuss their work, she added hastily, reminding herself not to make more of their relationship than it was.

While she thanked the Walkers for being such gracious hosts, Lydia was aware that Scott and Heather had stepped off to the side for a murmured conversation. It bothered Lydia that the twins seemed to be quarreling softly. She hoped it had nothing to do with her.

Scott said something else to his sister in a rather stern tone, then both of them pasted on smiles and turned to rejoin the others. "It was nice to see you again, Lydia," Heather said dutifully.

It was almost funny. Heather looked so much like a child who'd been reprimanded and ordered to be on her best behavior.

"Thank you, Heather," Lydia said with a completely straight face. "It was nice to see you, too."

Steve looked completely oblivious to any undertones. "We'll have to all get together sometime. Maybe we can go out for dinner or something."

"Oh, yes," Heather said, her smile almost glittering. "That would be lovely."

"We'll do that sometime." Scott's tone was the one people use when they said what courtesy expected of them. And then he placed a hand on Lydia's arm. "Ready, Lydia?"

She agreed gratefully, hoping she wouldn't have to deal with Scott's perplexing twin again.

They were in Scott's car headed back to Dallas when Lydia spoke again. "Well. That was interesting."

Scott chuckled wryly. "'Interesting' is a good word to describe my friends."

"I like them," she assured him. "They were all very nice."

"It's okay for you to exclude Alexis from that description. She's not one of my friends, and her behavior this evening wasn't at all nice."

"No," Lydia had to agree. "She was actually quite rude to Kelly and Shane, who went out of their way to be gracious hosts to her.''

''Of the women Cameron has dated in the past year—about a dozen, I would estimate—Alexis is my least favorite. Cam was apparently too distracted by her, um, physical attributes to notice that she's basically a—''

''I get the picture,'' Lydia cut in quickly.

Scott chuckled. ''At least that's over now. I doubt they'll see each other again after tonight.''

''I take it Cameron believes in playing the field.''

''You could say that. Nice guy—one of my closest friends—but not a good bet for a long-term relationship. He has an allergy to commitment. You might want to keep that in mind.''

Lydia lifted an eyebrow. ''Any particular reason?''

''Cameron can be very charming. I've known women to fall for him even when they knew better from the start.''

''Like your friend Amber?'' she hazarded.

"You heard about her, did you?"

"Your sister mentioned her—in context with her own matchmaking talent, I believe. She said she knew Cameron and Amber wouldn't work out and that she wished everyone had listened to her at the time. She added that she has a knack of knowing when a couple is wrong for each other. Oddly enough, she was looking directly at me when she said it."

Scott winced. "Sheer coincidence, I'm sure."

"Of course," she agreed without believing it any more than he did.

"Anyway, about Cameron..."

"He asked if I would mind answering DNA questions for him when he works on relevant news stories. I told him I would be happy to do so...a similar arrangement to the one I have with you," she added. Scott muttered something she didn't quite catch. She decided not to ask him to repeat it. Instead, she changed the subject. "Shane's ranch looked nice. I'd like to see it in the daylight sometime."

"It's a great place. He owns it with his father and stepmother, Jared and Cassie Walker. They and their teenage daughter, Molly, live in the main ranch house, which is about a quarter mile on down the road from Shane's place. They raise registered cattle and a few horses. They don't expect to get rich, but they're making enough to support themselves."

"Shane certainly looks the part of a rancher. The lean, tanned cowboy image suits him."

"He's cultivated it," Scott said with a quick grin. "You should see him decked out for a rodeo in his chaps and buckles."

Lydia pictured the result and nodded. "I'm sure he looks very dashing."

Scott cleared his throat. "I ride pretty well myself."

"Is that right?"

He nodded. "Don't let the sports car and lawyer-casual clothes fool you. At heart, I'm still a Texan."

"Have you competed in rodeo?"

"Er—yeah. Once. It wasn't pretty," he admitted ruefully.

Lydia laughed, and Scott joined in.

"I'm glad you came with me this evening, Lydia."

Her amusement faded. "Your sister wasn't pleased to see me. I'm not imagining it, Scott. She doesn't like me."

"She doesn't even know you."

"Nor does she want to. There's obviously something about me that bothers her."

"It's simply that she didn't personally select you. I'm afraid Heather's gotten rather clingy since our mother died unexpectedly a few months ago."

"I'm sorry. I didn't know."

He nodded to acknowledge the expression of sympathy. "It's left us without any other family except for a few relatives we never knew well. Even though she's with Steve now, she still wants to keep me close by. Picking out my dates for me is her way of keeping me under control, I guess."

He had just unwittingly confirmed her earlier speculation. "She's afraid the two of you will grow apart."

"That's ridiculous. We're twins, for Pete's

sake. Just because we have our own lives away from each other doesn't mean we're growing apart.''

''You lost your mother recently and Heather's getting married in a few months. That's a lot of change in a short time. It's only natural for her to want some things to stay the same.''

Scott nodded thoughtfully. ''Maybe you're right. I'll try to be more patient with her. But I'm not going to date her friends just to keep her feeling secure.''

Lydia kept her approval of that resolution to herself just in case he took it the wrong way. After all, it was hardly her business whom Scott dated.

''Still,'' she said, bothered that she had come between the twins when there was so little justification for it, ''you really should make it clear to her that you and I are only friends. There's no need to worry her unnecessarily.''

''I've never told her we were anything *but*

friends. I have no control over her vivid imagination.''

''But shouldn't you tell her—''

''I'm not telling her anything she doesn't need to know,'' Scott said firmly. ''And I expect her to be polite to you whenever she sees us together.''

Since Lydia didn't expect that to happen often—if ever again—she decided to let the comment pass.

''So now we're on for *your* sister's party,'' Scott commented.

She twisted her fingers in her lap. ''Maybe that's not such a good idea. I'd hate for things to become even more awkward between us and our sisters.''

Scott nodded pleasantly. ''Sure. No problem. If you'd rather spend the evening with Charlie's friend, Gary—''

''Okay, we're on,'' Lydia broke in, neatly trapped.

He laughed softly, his rather smug tone tempting her to punch his arm.

She seemed to have gotten herself involved

in something that was spiraling out of her control. Wouldn't it be easier to just stand firm and tell their siblings to butt out of their social lives?

It had seemed like a good idea at the beginning to have a friend who was a convenient "standby escort." She knew other platonic couples who had similar arrangements. But she wasn't sure it would be as easy for her and Scott. She was having to remind herself a bit too often that they weren't really "dating." That neither of them was interested in a relationship at this point. That she wasn't really a part of his group of friends. She shouldn't have to keep reminding herself of those things, she thought with a frown.

Scott insisted on walking Lydia to her door even though it was only upstairs from his own apartment, as she futilely pointed out. It made no difference. He remained by her side as she climbed the stairs.

"I'll call you later in the week," he said at her door. "Let me know when your sister schedules her housewarming party."

She nodded.

Scott chuckled and reached out to give her a quick hug. "Don't look so apprehensive, Lydia. Tonight went very well, on the whole. We can handle your sister's party."

Even knowing he was a "toucher" didn't keep her from becoming a bit flustered by the hug. Feeling her cheeks warm, she cleared her throat and awkwardly tucked a strand of hair behind her ears. "Well...good night, Scott."

He stood for a moment looking down at her, close enough that his breath ruffled her hair. Her stomach fluttered; she had to resist an impulse to press a hand to it. She was beginning to wonder if he was going to respond to her words when he finally spoke. "Good night, Lydia. Sleep well."

She nodded, not quite sure she trusted her voice, then slipped inside her apartment. She closed the door between them with a bit more haste than courtesy.

Lydia hadn't realized quite how dull her wardrobe had become until she was skimming through her closet Monday morning in preparation for work. "Black, black, navy, gray," she muttered, sliding hangers across the bar. "Don't I even own anything in red or green?"

She didn't know why she'd suddenly become aware of her fashion limitations. Clothes didn't usually matter that much to her as long as she was neat and generally coordinated. Larissa was the one who used clothes as a personality statement—bold and colorful and daring. Slipping into a knee-length navy skirt with a white shell and navy jacket, she told herself it was time for a shopping excursion. With the exception of the gown she'd bought for the charity auction, she hadn't been clothes shopping in quite a while.

This time she wouldn't take Larissa with her, she decided. Despite her sister's undeniable sense of style, she was too determined to try to dress Lydia like herself. She wouldn't mind having a friend go with her, but she couldn't think of anyone right offhand to call. Most of the women she knew were professional associates with whom she rarely socialized outside of the meetings and official gatherings where she usually saw them. It seemed that she'd neglected more than her wardrobe during her single-minded pursuit of her degrees and her career.

Maybe seeing Scott with his friends had started her thinking along these lines. They'd seemed so close. So comfortable together. She suspected they had their share of disagreements but would rally around without question if one of their own was in trouble.

Lydia had never belonged to a group like that. And she was keenly aware of that lack as she left for the job that had seemed so all-important to her for so long.

Because she had no classes that afternoon, Lydia decided to do a bit of shopping that very day. She needed some clothes. She had a few free hours to shop. She intended to get it done as quickly and efficiently as possible.

Scott spotted Lydia's car turning into the parking lot of their apartment complex just as he approached in his own car. He pulled in behind her, parking two spaces down.

"Hey," he drawled, climbing out from behind the wheel. "How's it going, Professor?"

"Hello, Scott." She opened the rear door of her car as she returned the greeting.

Gripping an attaché case filled with papers he planned to read later that evening, he circled behind her car, noting the number of packages piled on the back seat. "I see you've been shopping."

"Very perceptive of you." She stacked packages precariously in her arms, then reached for more.

"Looks like you bought out the store."

"Not completely."

Her juggling act was getting impressive. He watched in fascination as she added another bag to the pile. "Need any help?"

"I can get it." Steadying the stack with her chin, she reached for her purse. And promptly spilled everything else into the back seat again. She muttered a mild curse.

Laughing, Scott asked, "Are you sure you don't need help?"

Sighing, she brushed her hair out of her face and frowned at the mess in her car. "Maybe I could use a hand."

"I just happen to have one free."

They bent simultaneously to pick up a large, thick manila envelope that had fallen at her feet. They came within an inch of bumping heads, both of them almost stumbling in their effort to avoid the collision. Laughing again, Scott dropped his briefcase and reached out to catch her shoulders, steadying them both.

"And my day was going so well until now," Lydia said with a low moan, closing her eyes.

He feigned indignation. "Are you saying your day started falling apart when I showed up?"

She opened her eyes and smiled. "I certainly didn't mean to imply that."

"You really have a lovely smile," Scott murmured on impulse, admiring the little indentations at each corner of her mouth.

Her cheeks darkened. She moved a bit restlessly beneath his hands. ‘‘Um…thank you. We really should…’’

Her voice faded as if she’d forgotten exactly what it was they should be doing. They continued to kneel beside her car, his hands on her shoulders, their faces only inches apart.

Their mouths were very close, Scott couldn’t help noticing. He would only have to lower his head a very short distance—

‘‘Scott?’’

Her voice brought him back to his senses. What was he doing? Had he actually been thinking about kissing Lydia? That certainly wasn’t the sort of friendly, platonic relationship they’d agreed to.

But it might have been an interesting experience, he thought with a touch of regret. ‘‘Let me help you up.’’

She stepped away from him as soon as they were on their feet. Something about the flustered way she was acting made him wonder if the thought of a kiss had crossed her mind, as well.

Avoiding his eyes, she piled his arms with packages, then gathered the rest of her things. Scott caught a glimpse of several colorful garments beneath protective plastic coverings. "New clothes?"

"A few. My wardrobe was getting limited."

She matched her steps to his, keeping her eyes focused on the apartment building ahead of them. "How was your day? You're home earlier than usual, aren't you?"

He was rather surprised that she knew he usually arrived home much later. "Yes, actually, I am. I have some paperwork to concentrate on and there were too many distractions at the office. There's a meeting going on there that will probably run very late, and even though it doesn't involve me, people kept poking their heads in my office to tell me something."

Lydia nodded sympathetically. "That's the way it is at my office. There's always a student or fellow faculty member waiting to talk to me, and the phone rings off the hook, and the computer constantly tells me I have more e-mail.

Sometimes the only way I can get any work done is to lock myself in my apartment, turn off the phone, pull down the blinds and pretend to be out of town."

"That's sort of what I have in mind for this evening."

"Then I won't cause you any further delay." She balanced her load while she unlocked her door. "Thank you for helping me bring my things up."

"You're welcome."

Feeling as though she was brushing him off, he had the obstinate urge to linger—even though he'd told the truth about the amount of work he wanted to get done that evening.

"You can just pile those things on that chair," she said when they entered her living room.

He dumped the packages on the wing chair she'd indicated. "Have you talked to your sister since I saw you last?"

"Yes, she called yesterday."

"Has she made plans for her party yet?"

"She's thinking about Friday night at eight."

"Then unless something changes, I'll pick you up at seven-thirty."

Lydia cleared her throat and glanced down at her hands. "I know how busy you are, Scott. I've been thinking about this, and there's really no need for you to make time to go to my sister's party. Her friends are a little...well, eccentric...and it won't be at all like the quiet, comfortable evening with your friends. I've decided it's ridiculous for me to worry about Larissa's scheming. I'll just tell her very firmly that I'm not interested in meeting Charlie's friend, and that should put an end to it."

Were they really going to have to go through this argument again? Scott wondered why Lydia had suddenly become so nervous about taking him. She had said she enjoyed his company, so it wasn't that she didn't want to spend time with him—at least he hoped not. "I'd really like to go, if you don't mind. Spending an evening with a group of artists would be an interesting change of pace for me. I think it will be fun."

She looked doubtfully at him. "You think it will be *fun?*"

"Sure. I haven't had the opportunity to mingle with many artists. Usually, I hang out with lawyers, cowboys and corporate types. I always enjoy meeting people with different interests."

"Larissa's friends are definitely different," she murmured.

"I look forward to meeting them."

"Well...if you're sure."

"I'm quite sure." He didn't know why exactly he was so determined to go. While it was true that he thought an evening with artists might be interesting, he wasn't certain that was his primary motivation. And although he considered it a payback of sorts because Lydia had gone with him to the Walker ranch, he didn't think she would hold him to the obligation. Maybe he just wanted to spend more time with her. They were friends, he reminded himself. Friends enjoyed spending time together. Sharing experiences. Sharing an occasional hug, he added, remembering how nice it had felt to have his arm around her.

He supposed he should go. He had work to do, and so did she. So why did he find himself wanting to hang around just to talk to her a while longer, to watch the expressions crossing her face?

Startled by the unexpected turn his thoughts had taken, he shook his head slightly and stepped toward the door. ''I'll be seeing you, Lydia.''

''Let me get the door for you.''

She reached for the doorknob at the same moment he did. Their hands collided, his fingers sliding over hers. Impulsively, he tightened them, capturing her hand in his. ''I've got you now,'' he teased.

She smiled. ''And just what do you plan to do with me?''

Now *that* was an interesting question. He kept her hand in his while he considered it. She had pretty hands, he noted. Long fingers. Neat, oval nails.

''Um, Scott?''

He lifted his gaze from her pretty hand to her equally pretty blue eyes. ''Yes?''

''You were leaving?''

''Mmm. I'm going. In a minute.''

''Is there something else you want to say?''

''Something else I want to do,'' he corrected her.

''And that is?''

''This.'' Before she could guess his intentions—and before *he* could give it a second thought—he tugged at her hand, pulling her into his arms. Her lips parted to speak; he smothered whatever she might have said with his mouth.

He'd paid a lot of attention lately to her full, soft mouth. He'd found himself wondering how it would taste. And now he knew—pure heaven.

Chapter Five

Probably because he had taken her so completely by surprise, Lydia didn't resist Scott's kiss at first. He thought she was actually beginning to respond—her lips warmed and softened, moving just slightly against his—and then she seemed to come to her senses. She pulled away from him with a gasp, her eyes huge.

"What," she demanded, "was *that?*"

"That," he replied, "was curiosity. You're a scientist. You should understand the impulse to experiment."

She frowned. "I do my experimenting in my lab, not my living room."

Half-aroused and fully amused by her stern tone, he studied the high color in her cheeks and the temperamental glitter in her eyes. Outrage suited her, he decided. Passion would look even better on her. He didn't know where these thoughts were coming from or what had prompted his uncharacteristic behavior.

Lydia drew herself up and gave him a look he imagined she might have given one of her students who stepped out of line. In her chilliest, college-professor voice, she said, "I really think it would be better if we refrain from any further 'experimenting.' We've agreed not to cloud our comfortable friendship with potentially sticky complications."

"It was only a kiss, Lydia."

His wry reminder made her cheeks darken again. "I'm aware of that."

"A very nice kiss, actually."

"Yes...I mean, that isn't relevant."

Telling himself to leave before he ruined what had been a very pleasant association, he smiled and held up a hand in a conciliatory gesture. "You're right. I was out of line and I apologize. I won't say I regret it, but I do apologize," he added.

She seemed on the verge of snapping at him, but then she drew a deep breath and spoke in measured tones. "Thank you for helping me with my packages. Now, if you'll excuse me, we both have work to do this evening."

He nodded. "The one thing both of us always make time for is work."

"Let's just say it's the only thing I do well," she murmured, this time opening the door without interference from him.

"Somehow I'm beginning to doubt that," Scott muttered, finding himself suddenly in the hallway, her door closed firmly between them.

Lydia didn't see Scott during the days that passed after that wholly unexpected kiss at her door. Truth was, she very carefully avoided him that week, throwing herself totally into her work. But being out of sight did not mean Scott was out of mind. She thought of him all too often during those days, sometimes to the detriment of her concentration on more pressing matters.

She had replayed the kiss dozens of times in her mind and was still no closer to understanding what had motivated it. Had it truly been just a whim on Scott's part?

An "experiment," he'd called it. She wondered what he'd learned from it. Did he regret the impulsive action—or did he expect it to happen again?

She wasn't even sure what *her* answer to those questions would be. Did she regret that Scott had kissed her? Well, no, not exactly. It had been a very nice kiss—and, she had to admit, something she'd daydreamed about on more than one occasion.

Scott hadn't been the only one who'd been curious about what a kiss between them would be like. He was merely the one who'd given in first to the urge to find out.

As for whether she wanted it to happen again—she should probably say no. When she was in Scott's arms, the line between fantasy and reality became a bit too blurred, and that could prove dangerous to an admittedly vulnerable heart. It had seemed safe enough to go out with him as platonic friends. But if they were to start clouding the comfortable relationship with physical attraction—no matter how casual or temporary Scott considered it to be—she wasn't sure she could deal with that.

She had considered calling him and canceling the date for Larissa's party. She hadn't done so primarily because she hadn't known what to say to him. She decided instead to pretend nothing had happened between them Monday afternoon and hope Scott would go along with the charade.

When her doorbell rang at the appointed time Friday evening, she wondered for one panicky moment if she'd made a big mistake by letting this date stand. What would she say to him now? How was she supposed to act? What, if anything, did he want from her?

She wasn't even comfortable with what she had chosen to wear. One of the outfits she'd impulsively purchased Monday afternoon, it consisted of a thin, close-fitting red sweater and a long, straight wrap skirt of a silky black fabric printed with poppies. She wore chunky-heeled black shoes and onyx-and-silver jewelry. She'd thought the ensemble looked bright and cheery when she tried it on at the store. Now she wondered if the sweater was too tight, the plunging neckline too low. If the color was too bright, the style too young for her. She probably should have stayed with her usual selection of business suits and blazers.

Running a hand down the printed skirt, she opened the door in response to the second buzz of her doorbell.

She could tell that Scott took in every detail of her appearance in his first encompassing glance. "You look great," he said. "Red's a good color for you."

Compliments came easily to Scott, she reminded herself. It was part of the smooth, charming manner he had perfected. "Thank you," she said, refusing to be flattered.

"I like your hair that way, too. Very flattering."

She had swept the sides away from her face with small black clips. She would not let herself be pleased that he'd noticed. Nor would she dwell on how good *he* looked in his soft brown sweater and crisp khakis.

"You're sure you still want to go to this thing?" she asked him, giving him one last chance to change his mind.

"Wouldn't miss it for the world."

"Wish I could say the same," she muttered.

Scott laughed. "Lydia, it's a party, not a root canal."

"I've never minded going to the dentist. But Larissa's parties definitely cause me anxiety."

"They're not that bad, surely."

She shuddered dramatically in illustration. "You'll see. I'll spend the entire evening defending my decision to study science and not art, music or philosophy—all much more worthy pursuits, according to Larissa's friends. I'll be attacked by a few of them because scientific study has so often involved animal research—as if I were personally responsible for it. Someone will say my aura looks murky and someone else will want to read my palm or my cards or my toenails. And all of them will be sure to say they simply can't *believe* I'm Larissa's sister."

"An intolerant group, I take it?"

"Only of certain people," she said with a wry shrug.

"And what will they think about having a lawyer in their midst?"

"I can't imagine."

Looking completely undaunted, he laughed again and took her arm. "Let's go find out, shall we?"

Lydia felt a ripple of awareness go through her at the touch of his hand. And reminded herself that Larissa's exasperating friends were not all she had to worry about that evening.

The housewarming party was as noisy, rowdy and unconventional as Lydia had predicted. And as interesting as Scott had anticipated.

Larissa and Charlie had moved into a roomy, converted loft apartment in Dallas's

West End area. The large, high-ceilinged apartment was nearly filled with people. This group believed strongly in expressing themselves with their appearance; Scott saw several tattoos and unusually placed piercings. Lots of long, flowing, rainbow-colored hair—on both genders—and clothing colors ranging from neons to artistic black.

Snacks and beverages were plentiful, but everything was healthy, organic and vegetarian. The strongest drink available was an organically microbrewed ale; Scott decided to stick with a citrusy fruit punch. Fortunately, there were a few chocolate snacks available. ''We're vegetarians,'' Charlie murmured when Scott made the observation. ''Not masochists.''

Scott rather liked Charlie.

Wearing tangerine and black, Larissa swept through the room like a colorful tornado, touching everyone she encountered along the way. She towed someone behind her as she approached the corner where Scott, Lydia and Charlie visited. The man's eyes were almost hidden behind a mop of curly dark hair that tumbled forward onto his forehead. His face was round, as was the rest of him, though he wasn't particularly heavy, Scott noted, but rather soft, as if he didn't do much physical labor. His plaid cotton shirt flapped over faded jeans. Though it was very early in March and still cold and damp outside, he wore heavy leather sandals on his feet.

"Lydia," Larissa sang out, pulling the man to a stop in front of them, "here's someone I want you to meet. This is Gary Dunston, a new friend of Charlie's, now a new friend of mine. Gary, this is my sister, Lydia. Oh, and her friend, Scott Pearson," she added offhandedly.

Gary smiled a bit shyly at Lydia and then Scott. "Nice to meet you both."

"You and Lydia have a lot in common, actually," Larissa went on before either of them could respond. "I've told you she loves theater and books, and you, of course, love theater and own a bookstore. Why don't you compare notes while I show Scott my latest painting?"

Larissa had all the subtlety of a steamroller,

Scott thought wryly. She and Heather would probably bond instantly.

"Larissa—" Lydia began firmly.

"I would love to see your new painting," Scott cut in quickly, giving Larissa a smile. Something about this situation appealed to his sense of humor. And, besides, he wanted to score a few points with Lydia's sister.

Allowing himself to be towed away by Larissa, he glanced over his shoulder to send a grin toward Lydia, who glared back at him as if he had cravenly betrayed her.

The painting was in Larissa's studio, a big, multiwindowed, nearly empty room off the side of the main room. Scott examined the intriguingly arranged shapes and colors with interest. "Very nice," he said.

Larissa eyed him suspiciously. "You like it?"

"Very much. It reminds me of snorkeling in the Bahamas—all the bright colors and watery light and waving shapes."

She blinked rapidly, seemingly taken aback.

"Yes, I, um, painted this after Charlie and I got back from a Bahamas trip at Christmas."

"Is it for sale? I have a perfect place for it in my apartment."

"We can discuss that later. Did my sister tell you I don't like lawyers?"

Scott was more amused than offended by Larissa's deliberately blunt question. He turned away from the painting to face her. "No, she didn't mention it. But it's a sentiment many people share."

She studied his expression through her heavily darkened lashes. "That doesn't seem to bother you much."

"I've learned to live with it."

"Laughing all the way to the bank, hmm?"

She seemed to be trying to annoy him. She wasn't even being particularly subtle about it. But she wasn't succeeding. He merely shrugged and said, "I suppose some people might put it that way."

"I understand you and Lyddie have been seeing quite a lot of each other during the past few weeks," she prodded.

"We've attended a few parties together."

"Lydia has never been very fond of parties."

Scott shrugged. "Maybe she's learning to tolerate them."

"You, on the other hand, look like a man who enjoys a party."

Wondering just where she was going with this, he lifted an eyebrow. "What makes you say that?"

"Just an impression. Am I right?"

"There was a time when I spent most of my free time at various parties. Not so much now that I've gotten older and busier, but I still enjoy the occasional get-together."

She nodded as if he'd confirmed her guess. "So what do you see in Lydia?"

Was she implying that she couldn't imagine why he would be attracted to Lydia? If so, she was seriously underestimating her sister. "That's an odd question. Why *wouldn't* I want to spend time with Lydia?"

"To be honest, you seem to have very little

in common. You don't resonate in sync, if you know what I mean."

"I'm not sure I do," he replied dryly. "I've never been heavily into New Age terminology. And I think any 'resonating' that goes on between Lydia and me is no one else's business."

"So do I," Charlie said, giving his lover a stern look as he entered the studio in time to hear Scott's statement. "Larissa, you promised me you wouldn't embarrass your sister or her friend this evening."

She eyed Scott thoughtfully. "He's not embarrassed. A little annoyed, maybe, but not embarrassed."

"She means well," Charlie murmured apologetically to Scott. "She just isn't usually tactful about it."

"It's okay. I have an annoying sister of my own."

Charlie laughed. After a moment, Larissa smiled ruefully and shook her head. "I was just curious about what's going on between you and Lydia. She hasn't spent so much time with any guy in...well, in a long time. You can't blame me for wondering."

"Of course he can." Charlie gave her a fond smile as he slid an arm around her waist. "Leave the man alone, Larissa. Let him enjoy the party. Help yourself to the munchies, Scott. And ask Lydia if she wants to join you. That will give you an excuse to get her away from Gary. Last I heard, he was pretty much listing every title he carries in his bookstore. He's a really pleasant guy but not much of a conversationalist, I'm afraid."

"I'll do that. Thanks." He really did like Charlie, Scott thought as he nodded at Larissa and moved toward the doorway.

He heard Larissa burst into a defensive speech before he was even out of hearing range. "But, Charlie," she said, "I was only trying to find out..."

Scott didn't try to hear any more. He thought he knew exactly what Larissa had been trying to find out.

Lydia looked decidedly tense by the time Scott reached her.

"There's another section that might interest you as a scientist," Gary was saying earnestly when Scott stopped behind him. "It's a collection of books on West African healing practices. There are some fascinating discussions of the mind-body-earth connection that you would—"

"Excuse me." Taking pity on his date, Scott moved to her side. "I hate to interrupt, Lydia, but I thought you might be thirsty. I'm going over to the snack table. Can I bring you anything?"

"I'll go with you," she said eagerly, latching on to his arm. "It's been very nice talking to you, Gary. Perhaps I'll stop by your bookstore sometime."

"Yes, please do so. And, uh, bring your friend," he added with a less-than-enthusiastic look at Scott.

Scott gave him a bland smile. "I would be delighted."

"*Thank* you," Lydia breathed as they moved toward the snacks. "I was afraid he was going to start quoting passages to me next.

He seems very pleasant but totally obsessed with his bookstore inventory."

"Another workaholic." Scott chuckled. "You and I can both identify with that."

She groaned softly. "Do I sound that dull when I'm discussing microbes or DNA?"

"I have never found you in the least dull," he assured her, patting her hand where it rested on his arm.

"If you ever do hear me running on, feel free to kick me or something."

"It would be my pleasure."

She frowned at him. "You needn't sound quite so enthusiastic about it."

He laughed softly and reached for a snack plate.

"Lydia?" A very tall woman with gold-streaked hair and sapphire-blue eyes approached with a smile. "How nice to see you again."

Scott noted that the smile Lydia gave in return was a genuine one. "Cheyenne! It's been forever since I've seen you. How are you?"

"Fine, thank you. I haven't been in town

much during the past year. Working, you know.''

''Larissa told me your modeling career is going very well. That's wonderful.''

''Yes, it's been a great year. But the best thing that's happened to me lately is this,'' the striking model added, holding out her left hand to display an impressively sized diamond ring.

''You're engaged?'' Lydia's smile deepened. ''Congratulations. Who's the very fortunate man?''

''He's a photographer. I met him on a shoot in Italy last spring. We're getting married next summer.''

''That's wonderful news. I hope you'll be very happy.''

''I'm sure I will be. He's everything I ever dreamed of,'' Cheyenne gushed contentedly.

Remembering her manners, Lydia glanced contritely at Scott. ''I'm sorry, I'm being neglectful. Cheyenne, let me introduce you to my friend, Scott Pearson.''

Scott had already placed the woman. He wondered if she would remember him.

It seemed she did. Her dramatic eyes widened when she looked at him. "Well, if it isn't the hotshot attorney."

He smiled. "Hello, Cheyenne. It's very nice to see you again."

"You've met?" Lydia seemed surprised.

Cheyenne nodded. "We have a mutual friend. How is Paula, Scott?"

He lifted a shoulder. "I haven't seen her much lately, but she was fine last time I talked to her. I suppose you've heard she's moving to California in a couple of weeks?"

"No, I haven't. She's finally making the big move, hmm? She's been talking about it for years."

"She sold her house last week. Looks like she's really going to do it this time."

"I know you'll miss her. You've been friends for a long time."

Scott wondered what, if anything, Lydia made of the emphasis Cheyenne gave to the word "friends." "Yes, quite a while."

"I'll have to give her a call to wish her well with her move."

"I'm sure that would please her."

"Now, if you'll both excuse me, I've hardly had a chance to speak with Larissa this evening. I'm going to try to corner her for a few minutes to catch up."

"She's beautiful, isn't she?" Lydia murmured as they watched Cheyenne glide away.

"More striking than beautiful. Those eyes are incredible."

"And she moves with such grace." Lydia sighed wistfully. "I've envied the way she walks ever since Larissa introduced me to her three or four years ago, when they met through a yoga class."

Scott turned fully back to Lydia then. "You have absolutely no reason to envy Cheyenne. She has a model's walk, but you have a grace of your own. It's something I've always admired about you."

Her cheeks flushed. "I wasn't fishing for a compliment."

"I know you weren't. And I wasn't necessarily giving you one. Just making an observation."

Lydia cleared her throat. "Those strawberries look good, don't they? I believe I'll have one."

The party was still in full swing when Lydia and Scott left—and would go on for several more hours, Lydia suspected. She, for one, was relieved to climb into Scott's car and be surrounded by quiet rather than chaos. She sighed. "I'm so glad that's over."

Scott seemed amused as he started the engine. "It wasn't that bad."

She looked at him with raised eyebrows. "You didn't seem to feel that way when R. C. Polk pinned you to the wall and tried to get you to agree that he should sue the *Morning Star* art critic for savaging his work."

"He didn't exactly pin me to the wall. He was just passionate about his indignation. I think I convinced him that a critic has the right to express his opinions without being sued for doing so."

"I heard you suggest that R.C. write a strongly worded letter to the editor. He probably will—a whole ream of letters, more likely.''

''A perfectly legitimate way to express his own opinions of the art critic's taste.''

Lydia relaxed against the back of her seat, watching the streetlights pass by through the windshield. ''You probably made a friend for life when you told R.C. that most art critics seem to be myopic reactionaries who wouldn't know true genius if it bit them in their posteriors.''

Scott laughed. ''I didn't actually say that. I merely agreed with him when *he* said it. He seemed to expect me to.''

Lydia abruptly changed the subject. ''Are you really buying Larissa's new painting?''

''*Atlantis Dawn?* Yes, I am. As soon as I convince her to sell it to me, of course.''

She looked at him doubtfully. ''Do you really want it or are you buying it just to be nice to my sister?''

''Trust me, I wouldn't spend that much just to impress your sister. It's a beautiful painting. I wanted it as soon as I saw it.''

She couldn't help but be proud. "Larissa is very talented, isn't she? I'm so glad her work is finally getting the attention it deserves."

Scott's attention was distracted for a moment by the demands of his driving. They rode in companionable silence while Lydia thought about the party. She wondered if Scott had really enjoyed the evening. And she wondered who Paula was and what Cheyenne's tone had signified when she spoke of the woman to Scott.

Since she couldn't think of a tactful way to find out, she asked instead, "What did Larissa say to you when she dragged you into her studio? She wasn't just trying to sell you a painting, was she?"

"Mostly she wanted to tell me she doesn't like lawyers."

Lydia groaned and covered her face with a hand, appalled by her sister's lack of manners. "Oh. Sorry."

"And then she asked whether you and I have been resonating together."

Dropping her hand to her lap, she whipped

her head around to stare at him. "She asked you *what?*"

His grin was lopsided, displaying his slash of dimple. "I can't be sure of the exact wording, but it was something like that."

"What is it supposed to mean?"

"I think she was trying to find out if we're sleeping together."

"Oh, my God. I'll strangle her."

Scott laughed in response to her threat. "She really was a bit more subtle than that. You should probably let her live."

"What did you tell her?"

"The truth, of course. That we're having a mad, passionate affair involving lots of hot, kinky—"

"Scott!"

His laughter filled the snug confines of the sports car. "Chill out, Lydia. I told her our relationship is none of her business."

The reassurance didn't make her feel much better. She hadn't been this embarrassed in a long time. She couldn't believe she had allowed herself to be put in this situation. She knew what Larissa was like—why had she baited her by parading Scott in front of her?

"It's no big deal, Lydia. Larissa was just being a nosy sister—much like my own."

"We should never have attempted to outmaneuver either of them. Now they're both even more determined to interfere in our lives."

"Okay, be honest," he chided her. "Would you really rather have spent the evening with Bookstore Gary? He looked at you as if he wanted to put you behind glass like a rare first edition. And he didn't seem the type to take a hint easily. The only reason he backed off this evening is because I was there with you."

"I could have handled him."

"I'm sure you could. Still, it was easier because I was there. Just as your presence with me at the ranch prevented Heather from bringing someone to meet me last weekend."

She rubbed her temples, suddenly weary. "At least it's over now. Three parties in three weeks is enough. There's nothing else on my social calendar for a while. I can get back to work.''

``You really think Larissa will give up so easily?''

``She has no choice. She knows my work comes first.''

Scott made a sound she couldn't quite interpret, then remained quiet as he turned the car into their parking lot. He didn't speak again until he had parked in his usual space. ``Next time we get together, let's make it just us, shall we?''

She quickly reminded herself of the times they'd gotten together before, just the two of them. ``Yes, we'll have to do that sometime. We've never had a chance to discuss that article about laboratory contamination.''

``Actually, I didn't...'' He paused, then smiled a bit wryly. ``Yeah, that would be great.''

She didn't even try to talk him out of walking her to her door this time since she knew she would be wasting her breath. Scott Pearson was a gentleman down to his manicured nails.

And yet there was nothing gentlemanly about the way he looked at her when he turned to her at her door.

She gulped and reached for the doorknob. "Well...good night."

He detained her with a hand on her arm. "It is customary to conclude a date with a good-night kiss."

"But this wasn't a real date," she reminded him.

He lifted a hand to trace her jaw with his fingertips. "It felt pretty real to me."

"Scott..."

"Am I complicating things again?"

She couldn't seem to stop staring at his mouth, which was so close to her own. "Yes."

"Want me to stop?"

No, she almost said.

"Yes," she made herself say instead.

"Liar," he murmured with a soft laugh. And slid his hand behind her head to pull her mouth to his.

Chapter Six

Lydia had told herself this wasn't going to happen again. She had promised herself that, if it did, she wouldn't respond. She had made a solemn vow to herself not to get lost in this fantasy Scott had created for them.

Even as her hands slid up his chest to clench at his shoulders, she told herself she had to stop this. Even as her lips softened and parted, she tried to find the strength to draw away. And even as he drew her closer until she was pressed snugly against him, she felt herself getting utterly lost....

She wasn't the one who brought the long, thorough kiss to an end. It was Scott who finally lifted his head, slowly, lingeringly, breaking the embrace. He drew a deep, unsteady breath, his eyes dark green as he gazed down at her. For once, there was no evidence of lazy amusement on his face.

She stared up at him, unable to find the voice to speak even if she had known what to say.

Larissa, she thought, would have handled this moment with poise, humor, confidence. She would have known what to say to break the awkwardness, to bring the interlude to an end…or, maybe, if she had desired, to carry it further. She wouldn't have just stood there, staring stupidly up at him, feeling as if her head had been emptied of all coherent thought.

This was one of the times when Lydia wished she was more like her sister.

Scott cleared his throat. ''So maybe we could get together tomorrow? For dinner or something, I mean. We could talk about that lab contamination article," he added as if he'd just remembered it.

Not a good idea, she thought, gradually finding her way back to reality. Finally regaining her voice, she spoke with a firmness that came with an effort. "Thank you, but I have a lot of work to do. I really should get back to it."

For just a moment, he looked as if he would have liked to argue, but then he nodded. "I understand. I've been neglecting my own work a bit lately. I suppose I'd better get back to the grind myself."

"We agreed that neither of us really has time to date right now," she reminded him.

"Right." He ran a hand through his hair and, to her relief, took a step back from her. Somehow it seemed easier to breathe with a few more inches of space between them. "So," he said, "I'll call you sometime."

She nodded. "Please do."

Meaningless pleasantries, she thought. It was the first time she and Scott had resorted to them. It had been so much more comfortable between them before they'd messed everything up with dates and kisses. She should have remembered how often that had happened to her with other men who should never have tried to be more than friends with her.

Before things could get even more awkward and uncomfortable, she opened her door and slipped inside, closing it quietly but firmly between them.

As she turned on the overhead light, a stack of paperwork piled on her coffee table caught her eye, reminding her of the responsibilities always waiting for her. "Playtime's over," she murmured. "It's back to work for you now."

But it had been rather nice while it had lasted, she thought wistfully.

Lydia didn't hear from Scott—nor did she expect to—for the remainder of the weekend. She *was* surprised to receive a delivery of flowers at her office on Monday afternoon, a beautiful bouquet of white roses in a pretty, cut-glass vase. She dug through the blossoms looking for a note, but the only card she found bore only her name and delivery address.

She frowned at the arrangement in mingled pleasure and bemusement. Why hadn't Scott enclosed a card? Had he been so confident she would know who sent it? What message had he been trying to send?

Or *had* he sent it? But if not Scott, then who?

She groaned and rubbed her temples with the tips of her fingers. She hadn't had much sleep during the past two nights, having spent too many hours staring at the ceiling and seeing there an imaginary replay of that kiss outside her door. While she had indulged in secret fantasies of kissing Scott before, they had been pleasant, comfortable daydreams that seemed safe enough. But there had been nothing safe about the real thing. Nothing in the least comfortable about the feelings it aroused in her.

Someone hesitated in her open doorway. "Ms. McKinley?"

Pulling her gaze from the flowers to the young woman who'd spoken, Lydia thrust thoughts of Scott to the back of her mind. "Hello, Jessica. Can I help you?"

"It's about the assignment you gave in class this morning. I'm not really sure what you want our focus to be."

Lydia had explained the assignment in detail. Twice. And she had noticed even while doing so that Jessica had been paying more attention to the broad-shouldered young athlete in the seat beside her than to what Lydia was saying.

Drawing on her strained patience, she waved toward the chair on the other side of her desk. "I have five minutes before my next class. I'll go over it once quickly, but that's all I can give you. And it might help you in class if you chose a seat a bit farther from Mr. Sherman."

The young woman blushed rosily. "Thank you, Ms. McKinley. I'll try to pay closer attention from now on."

Since her own concentration had been adversely affected by a man that day, Lydia didn't feel as though she had much right to criticize Jessica.

* * *

"Scott? Were you actually going to play those cards or just sit and contemplate them for a while?"

Scott blinked, then frowned at Cameron, who sat across the table impatiently drumming his fingers. "I'm thinking."

"Yeah, but are you thinking about poker?"

"Leave the guy alone, Cam," Shane drawled, glancing up from his own hand. "As badly as he's playing tonight, the rest of us are benefiting from his inattention. I've already made twenty bucks off him."

"I always like playing poker with a lovesick dude," Michael agreed cheerfully, admiring the tidy stack of plastic chips in front of him. "It's hard for a guy to think with his head and his groin all at the same time."

"All right, that's enough," Scott growled, finding little amusement in their teasing. "As it happens, I've been distracted by a new case at work."

It was a lie, of course. A probably futile attempt to save face in front of his friends. He hated to admit he had spent the past week moping over Lydia like an infatuated teenager.

He didn't know why he couldn't seem to get her out of his mind lately. He'd known her for months without becoming obsessed with her before. He'd always admired her, had always found her attractive, had always enjoyed spending time with her. But it had been easy before. Comfortable. Casual. Why had that changed just because they'd shared a couple of kisses?

Was it simply ego? Had it stung his pride that Lydia didn't seem to be as deeply affected as he had been? That she had so coolly turned him down while his head was still spinning from a kiss that had shaken him to his boots?

A gusty sigh sounded from the other side of the table. "Call or fold, Pearson."

"Uh…call." Scott threw some chips on the table. Minutes later, he scowled when Shane scooped them up. "Oh, man. I'd better quit while I'm behind."

"Definitely not your night for poker, pal."

Shane stacked his chips and grinned lazily at Scott. "Something on your mind?"

"Some*one,* you mean," Michael murmured. "The pretty professor, perhaps?"

"Any of those brownies left?" Scott pushed his chair from Michael's kitchen table where they'd gathered to play poker while Kelly and Judy attended a baby shower for Shane's cousin, Brynn D'Alessandro.

"Ah. He's avoiding the subject." Michael nodded smugly. "The boy's got a case."

"Don't be an ass," Scott snapped, snatching one of the brownies Judy had made for them and plopping back into his seat. "Lydia and I are just friends."

"I, for one, am glad to hear that," Cameron murmured, reaching for his beer.

Scott frowned, trying to remember how many beers Cameron had had that evening. For the past year or so—ever since the inevitable but painful breakup with Amber—Cameron had been drinking harder, taking more risks, caring about little beyond his newspaper work and his small circle of longtime friends.

Estranged from his family, he was spending more and more time alone. When he did go out, he seemed to deliberately date women he didn't even particularly like. Scott suspected that Cameron was trying to keep anyone else from being hurt by his inability to commit to a permanent relationship. The whole gang was worried about Cameron, but he kept assuring them he was fine and didn't need their concern.

"Why are you glad to hear that Lydia and I are just friends?" Scott asked curiously.

Cameron's smile had a wicked edge to it. "If you're just friends, then you won't mind if *I* spend time with her. For research purposes, of course."

Scott had thought it might be a good idea for Cameron to spend time with a nice woman. He hadn't meant Lydia.

Refusing to let himself take Cameron's bait—as tempting as it was to do so—Scott took a bite of the brownie and mumbled around it, "That's between you and Lydia."

"I've got to admit, I've never seen a scientist with legs like hers," Cameron said.

"Sexist remark," Shane commented, shuffling cards. "Kelly would bite your head off if she heard you."

With a smile that looked more like the "old" Cam, he shrugged. "You're right. And I suppose I would deserve it. But Lydia does have great legs. Don't you think so, Scott?"

Scott had no intention of discussing Lydia's legs—great as they were—with these clowns. "Are we going to gossip or play poker?"

"Gossip works for me," Michael answered cheerfully. "How come you and Lydia are only friends, Scott? She seems perfect for you."

"Now you sound like my matchmaking sister. Except that she would rather fix me up with someone else."

"Heather doesn't like Lydia?" Shane looked surprised. "How come?"

"Beats the hell out of me. She said something about Lydia reminding her of Paula. Which is ridiculous, of course."

Michael shook his head. ''Lydia's nothing like Paula.''

''Other than the fact that they're both attractive, strong-willed, independent women with minds and lives of their own, they're nothing at all alike,'' Cam murmured.

Scott shook his head. ''Take it from someone who knows them both—they're very different.''

While Scott liked both women very much, he thought of them as almost complete opposites. Forty-year-old Paula had been married and divorced three times and was always on the lookout for her next rich husband. She *was* independent and self-sufficient, but her idea of taking care of herself was to marry well. She had confided to Scott that, contrary to what most people thought of her, she didn't go into the marriages with the intention of divorcing for alimony. She had even signed prenuptial agreements for her last two marriages, taking very little away with her after her divorces. Could she help it, she had asked ruefully with self-deprecating humor, if men—even her ex-husbands—insisted on giving her money and gifts?

Not that he was in a league with her wealthy exes, but Scott had always rather enjoyed giving Paula gifts himself. She always seemed so utterly delighted with them. He knew she was self-centered and materialistic and terminally restless when it came to staying too long in one place or with one man. But he'd had a great time with her while it lasted.

Despite Heather's fears about the woman she despised at first sight, Scott had never entertained thoughts of a longtime involvement with Paula. She had been what he needed at the time—an ego boost after a painful disaster of a relationship—and maybe he'd served the same purpose for her. They'd ended the affair quite congenially, and he wished her well with her new adventures.

He wasn't sure it would be possible to have such a pleasantly uncomplicated relationship with Lydia.

Lydia was more serious than Paula, more focused, less social. Her sense of humor was dryer, her sexuality more subtle. Lydia, Scott thought, was a woman who could almost make a man forget that he didn't have the time or inclination for a full-blown relationship. Not that it would do the guy any good. She'd made it clear enough that her own work came first with her.

"You going to let Heather keep you from seeing Lydia?" Michael wanted to know.

Scott shook his head. "I make my own decisions. But seriously, guys, there's nothing going on between Lydia and me. We're just friends."

"That's what I said about Kelly," Shane observed. "Right up until the day I proposed to her in front of my entire family."

Scott frowned repressively at him. "That isn't the case here."

He noted that none of his friends seemed convinced by his disclaimer.

A week and a half after Larissa's housewarming party, Lydia met her sister and their friend Cheyenne for lunch at a tearoom near the university. It was Cheyenne's last day in Dallas for a while, and she'd expressed a wish for one quiet visit with the McKinley sisters.

"We hardly had a chance to talk at the party," she said as they settled behind the various salads they had ordered for lunch.

"I always find it difficult to have conversations at parties," Lydia agreed. "I prefer more intimate get-togethers like this."

Larissa raised an eyebrow. "I happen to think that was a great party."

"Of course it was." Cheyenne smiled and patted Larissa's arm. "A truly great party. But this is nice, too, just the three of us."

Appeased, Larissa nodded and stuck her fork into her pasta salad.

Cheyenne turned then to Lydia. "I was so surprised when you came to the party with Scott Pearson. Have the two of you been seeing each other long?"

"We live in the same apartment building," Lydia hedged, aware of Larissa's sudden frown. "We've only been out together a few times."

"How long have *you* known him, Cheyenne?" Larissa inquired.

"I met him more than a year ago. He was involved then with a woman I know through my parents' country club. He and Paula were quite an item for a while."

"I've told Lydia that I'm not sure he's right for her," Larissa confided. "He's just so…smooth. Polished. I wouldn't be at all surprised to hear that he has political aspirations."

"I wouldn't know about that. I really didn't know him all that well. I just saw him at a few parties with Paula. He always seemed nice enough, if rather…"

"Rather *what?*" Larissa demanded when Cheyenne gave Lydia a glance and allowed her voice to trail off.

"Well…I suppose you said it best, Larissa. The guy's smooth. I always wondered if there was anything at all real beneath his pretty surface."

Larissa pounced on Cheyenne's words with alacrity. "There you go, Lyddie. Cheyenne agrees with me—and you've always said Chey was a good judge of people, right?''

''Well, yes, but—''

''I bet this guy broke your friend's heart, Cheyenne. And now he's moved on to my sister.''

Lydia rolled her eyes and started to protest, but Cheyenne spoke first with a little laugh. ''I doubt very seriously that any hearts were broken between Scott and Paula. Their relationship wasn't that serious. Paula's probably ten years older than Scott. Everyone knew they were just having a good time until something better came along. They were together for sex and laughs, and neither of them pretended to want anything more from each other. It was a relationship of convenience, not commitment.''

Convenience, Lydia thought with a sudden hollow feeling. The same type of arrangement Scott had proposed to her, though the subject of sex hadn't actually come up. Was that where he'd been headed with those kisses? Had he been auditioning her to be his next "convenient" friend? It didn't sound as though she had much in common with Paula, but she'd made it clear to Scott that she wasn't looking for a serious relationship right now. Had that been her chief attraction for him?

She hadn't heard from him during the ten days that had passed since Larissa's party—since she had turned down his invitation for dinner the next evening. Maybe he'd decided she wouldn't be so "convenient," after all.

"I've been trying to convince Lydia to go out with Charlie's friend, Gary," Larissa said to Cheyenne. "They seem like a much better match to me. You met Gary at the party, didn't you? He certainly seemed taken with Lydia. He's asked Charlie about her several times since."

"Gary?" Cheyenne frowned a moment, then nodded. "Oh, yes, I remember. The bookstore owner."

"Right. Charlie and I haven't known him very long, but he's really nice. He's a little shy and awkward when you first meet him, but once you get him talking about something other than his inventory, he's really a very interesting guy. Very sweet."

Cheyenne shook her head with a slight frown. "I really didn't talk to him long enough to form an opinion."

Lydia decided she'd had enough of this particular conversation. "Tell us about *your* life, Cheyenne. I want to hear all about your fiancé and your wedding plans. Where will you live after the wedding? Will you be able to come back to Dallas often?"

Cheyenne was distracted easily enough by Lydia's change of subject. She launched into an excited discussion of her upcoming plans, encouraged by more questions from Lydia. Larissa, of course, had to go along for courtesy's sake, but Lydia knew her reprieve was only temporary. Armed with Cheyenne's concurring reservations about Scott, Larissa would be even more determined to steer Lydia away from him.

When the subject did come back up, Lydia intended to make it clear to her sister that there was no reason to worry. There was absolutely nothing going on between her and Scott, nor was there likely to be. And that was exactly what Lydia wanted.

Right? she asked herself.

Then sighed wistfully into her salad.

There were flowers waiting for her when Lydia returned to her office after lunch with Larissa and Cheyenne. Roses again; pink, this time. And, again, there was no card enclosed with the delivery.

Lydia set her purse on her desk, shaking her head as she stared at the flowers in exasperation. Why did Scott keep sending her roses? Why didn't he at least send a card to give her a clue to his purpose?

She realized guiltily that she had never acknowledged the last delivery. She'd thought she would run into him at the apartment complex and could work it in then, but she hadn't seen him. Maybe she hadn't looked hard enough? Still flustered by the kiss that had so thoroughly shaken her after Larissa's party, she had been reluctant to call him. What if he misinterpreted her making the first move?

And yet he'd sent her flowers once more. Why?

Not that she was immune to the gesture. She couldn't help but be a bit flattered by his attentions. She couldn't even remember the last time a man had given her flowers—and now Scott had done so three times in as many weeks. But she couldn't stop wondering—just what did he want in return? And was she really interested in having the same sort of relationship with him that he and Paula had had?

"Sex and laughs," Cheyenne had called it. Lydia wasn't particularly comfortable with either option.

Chapter Seven

Eight o'clock Thursday evening, and Scott was still at his office, sitting behind a pile of papers he was a long way from working his way through. Dropping the remains of a dry take-out sandwich into his overflowing waste-basket, he pushed a hand wearily through his hair and considered escape. Maybe he could finish this tomorrow—but no. He had too many other projects due tomorrow. Getting behind now would only throw him behind for the rest of the week—and that was no way to earn a partnership.

So, he had another couple of hours to put in before he could rest tonight. But it wouldn't hurt to take a very brief break, he thought. He reached for the phone—something he'd been wanting to do for the past two hours.

Lydia picked up on the second ring, her voice sounding distracted, as if she, too, had been concentrating deeply on something else.

"Hi," he said. "It's Scott."

Her voice changed. Was it wariness he heard now? If so, why? "Um, hello. What can I do for you?" she asked.

He remembered a bit wryly that she'd told him she wasn't very good at making small talk. But her rather brusque, straight-to-business tone wasn't making this particular call any easier. "I was just taking a short break from work. I have a mountain of paperwork to get through this evening, but I thought I'd take a minute to see how you're doing."

"Are you at home?"

"No, still at the office. I needed access to my files and equipment here. It'll probably be another couple of hours before I can get away."

"Have you had dinner?"

He glanced toward the wastebasket. "Sort of."

"Has it occurred to you that your sister could be right about your working too hard?" she asked wryly.

"Mmm. And just what were *you* doing when I called, Professor?"

She cleared her throat. "Um...working on my thesis."

"And how much longer will you be at it this evening?"

"I was just about to put it away," she said sanctimoniously. And then added with rueful humor, "I have a stack of papers to grade yet tonight."

"Right. So *who* works too hard?"

"We both do, I suppose."

"Which is part of the reason I called." He took a quick breath, oddly nervous. "How'd you like to take a few hours off and see a movie with me this weekend? I'll even let you select a chick flick rather than a shoot-'em-up."

"I happen to like the occasional shoot-'em-up," she replied, making him smile. But then his smile faded when she added, "Thank you for the offer, but I'll have to decline. I'll be out of town this weekend for a microbiology convention."

"Oh." He frowned, unexpectedly disappointed with her answer. "Well...some other time, then?"

"Of course." Her reply was just a bit too perfunctory.

"Funny how we can live in the same apartment building and go so long without even seeing each other, isn't it?"

"Not so odd when you consider how little time either of us spends in our apartment."

"True."

"Which reminds me...I haven't even had a chance to thank you for the roses."

The roses? Scott lifted an eyebrow in surprise. He was quite sure she *had* thanked him when he'd given her the roses before the Valentine's Day charity affair weeks ago. What made her bring them up again now? "Yeah, sure. You're still welcome. Why—"

"I suppose it was obvious to you that I love roses. But really, Scott, there's no—"

Her rather confusing speech was interrupted when his other line buzzed. Since he was expecting a call from a colleague, he sighed and interrupted her. "Lydia, I'm sorry, I have a call coming in and I—"

"No problem. I have to get back to work myself," she said quickly.

"So I'll see you around, okay? Good luck with your conference."

"Thank you. And, Scott...?"

"Yes?"

"Get some rest."

He smiled. "I will. You, too. Good night, Lydia."

He disconnected and took the other call, switching into work mode. He couldn't help noticing that it took more effort than usual to keep his concentration on business rather than the frustrating and somewhat baffling conversation he'd just had with Lydia.

Exhausted as always after a weekend conference, Lydia threw her luggage on the bed and gratefully kicked off her shoes on Sunday afternoon. Her answering machine blinked to indicate messages. Tempted to ignore it a while longer, she made herself punch the play button just in case there was anything important she should attend to.

The first three messages were trivial. She listened to them while she unpacked, then promptly forgot them. The fourth message made her pause, a bundle of clothes in her arms.

"Lydia. This is Gary Dunston. Charlie's friend? We met at Charlie and Larissa's housewarming party. I'm the bookstore owner."

"Yes, I remember," she murmured, becoming impatient. "What do you want?"

"Anyway," he continued, "Larissa gave me your number. I hope you don't mind. She suggested I call you."

"I'll definitely strangle her," Lydia grumbled.

"Um—there's this thing. A reception and book signing at my store for a visiting author—he wrote *Microbe Mythologies,* which made me think of you, of course. Anyway, it's next Friday night and I thought, maybe, you'd like to come? As my guest?"

Some people might have found his shy, awkward stumbling rather endearing. Lydia was annoyed with herself for being so critical of him. Not every man could be as smooth and polished as Scott Pearson, she reminded herself. Then winced as she remembered how often Larissa had used those same adjectives in her less-than-flattering descriptions of Scott.

Gary completed his invitation by reciting his telephone number and asking Lydia to give him a call when she had time. She scribbled the number on the notepad she kept by the phone. She stared at it, wondering what she would say if she dialed it.

She really wasn't interested in going out with Gary. He seemed like a perfectly pleasant fellow, but she had no desire to spend time with him. She had so little spare time and she didn't want to spend it making stilted conversation with a man who just didn't excite her.

And then she groaned and covered her face with her hands. Since when had it mattered whether a man excited her or not? She'd dated infrequently during the past couple of years because she hadn't had time, not because she'd been waiting to be excited. If excitement was what she was looking for, she would have made more time to spend with Scott.

She really should just stick to her work, she told herself. She was good at that. She understood that. And she didn't have to be concerned about hurting someone's feelings at work—or being hurt in return.

She'd been spending entirely too much time thinking about Scott and his friends. Every time she'd tried to fit in with people from outside her academic world in the past, she'd been hurt. Her heart still bore a few scars from a man who'd professed to love her but had found someone more ‘‘fun’’ while Lydia was working toward her master’s degree.

She should probably accept Gary’s invitation. It would be the gracious thing to do and would help get her mind off Scott and whatever it was he wanted from her. And it would make Larissa happy—not that she particularly cared about *that,* since Larissa had gone about this whole fix-up in such an underhanded way.

Or maybe, she thought with a sigh, flopping backward onto her bed, she should just move to the Antarctic. She could study frozen microbes and socialize with penguins—all in all much less stressful than trying to understand Scott and stay one step ahead of Larissa.

‘‘I really appreciate your meeting me like this,’’ Cameron North said to Lydia over dinner at Vittorio’s Wednesday evening.

She smiled politely at the handsome blond man on the other side of the table for two. ‘‘You just happened to catch me when I have a couple of hours free before an evening class.

I thought I was going to have to grab a burger for dinner. This is much nicer.''

He slid a file folder across the table toward her. ''This is the story I was telling you about. A local attorney says he has DNA evidence that can clear his new client who's on death row. The circumstantial evidence against the guy was so strong that a jury convicted him unanimously after only an hour's deliberation. Now this lawyer says he's got fifteen-year-old blood samples from the crime scene that prove his guy's innocence. What do you think? Is it possible?''

''Certainly. There have been quite a few cases recently in which modern DNA testing has been useful in answering old crime questions. Fifteen years isn't really so long in comparison with some of the other more spectacular cases I've studied.''

''So will you look over these copies and give me your first impression of the guy's argument? He's having trouble getting attention from people who have the power to reopen the case, and he's hoping publicity can help him.

But before I spend much time on this, I'd like to know there's a reasonable chance he knows what he's talking about.''

''I'd be happy to look over your file, but you must understand that I'm no expert at forensic DNA. I've studied it and I discuss it in my undergraduate classes, but only on a rather general level.''

''Scott's consulted with you.''

''We've had a few friendly, casual discussions—question-and-answer sessions mostly. He hasn't officially consulted with me on any specific cases. I'm more like his volunteer DNA tutor.''

Cameron smiled. ''Scott told me you have a talent for explaining complex subjects in simple, easy-to-understand terms. Considering my science background, I need something on a level with DNA for Dummies.''

She laughed. ''I take it you aren't a science reporter?''

''Political corruption and white-collar crime have been more my usual style. But this one intrigued me, especially since you so generously volunteered to answer questions for me.''

''I hope I can be of help to you. I'll look through the file after my class this evening and get back to you sometime tomorrow.''

He nodded. ''The numbers where you can reach me are in the folder. I really appreciate this, Lydia.''

''You're welcome.'' She took a bite of her pasta, thinking that at least she ate well from her volunteer consulting.

''So, have you seen Scott lately? He's been so tied up at work that I haven't had a chance to catch up with him.''

She shook her head and looked down at her plate. ''No, I haven't seen him in a while. He and I have both been busy.''

''I'd make a comment that he works too much, but since I've been accused of the same thing lately, I guess I'd better not.''

''Yes, I get the same criticism.''

Cameron shrugged. ''If you like your work, why wouldn't you want to spend time doing it? People with spouses and kids have obligations at home, of course, but what are we singles supposed to do with our time? A person can only attend so many parties.''

''Exactly.'' Lydia thought he'd phrased that very well. ''I enjoy my work and my studies. I don't know why people get so bent out of shape because I want to spend time at them.''

''I know the feeling.'' Cameron's mouth twisted. ''If I spend too much leisure time, I'm considered a playboy. Too much time on the job and I'm accused of being a workaholic. A guy just can't win.''

''You having dessert tonight, Cam?'' the handsome young man who'd been serving them asked, pausing beside the table.

''Lydia?'' Cameron inquired.

''No, thank you. I have to get to my class.''

''Nothing for me, either, Nick. I'll take the check now.''

The young man nodded. ''I'll be right back.''

''You seem to be a popular customer here,'' Lydia commented, thinking of how many times he'd been greeted by restaurant employees since their arrival.

"I eat here a lot. The place is owned by the D'Alessandro family. The D'Alessandros have a family connection to my buddy, Shane Walker. Shane and I used to come here when we were broke college students and we could usually wheedle a few snacks out of the owner and his wife."

"Now why doesn't *that* surprise me?" Lydia suspected that Cameron had "wheedled" quite a few favors in his time. Along with Shane Walker's sexy cowboy charm, the pair was probably darned near irresistible. She wondered idly how many hearts had been broken when Shane had married Kelly.

Carrying her purse and the folder he'd brought, Lydia walked at Cameron's side toward the exit. He reached out to steady her when an incoming customer brushed rather roughly against her.

"Jerk," he muttered beneath his breath, glaring after the rude patron. "You okay, Lydia?"

She nodded. "He just bumped my arm."

Cameron ushered her out the door, his hand still casually resting at her waist as he talked. "Listen, if you don't have time to get to this stuff tonight, feel free to take another day, okay? I told the lawyer I'd get back to him by the end of the week, so we've got—"

He suddenly stopped talking as they stepped out into the cool, mid-March evening.

Lydia had been looking up at Cameron while he talked. When he went silent, she followed his gaze to see what had captured his attention so abruptly. And then she swallowed.

Scott Pearson stood in front of her, looking with a frown at Cameron's hand, which still lay against Lydia's waist. Scott didn't look at all happy to see them, Lydia couldn't help noticing. In fact, he looked downright displeased.

Cameron spoke first, breaking the brief, tense silence. "Hey, Scott. We were just talking about you. How's it going?"

"Fine." Scott lifted his gaze to Lydia's face. "How was your convention?"

Shifting subtly away from Cameron to break

the contact between them, she nodded. ''It was very interesting.''

''I see. So...you've been consulting for Cameron today?''

''She's very generously helping me with a story I'm researching,'' Cameron explained.

''Lydia's always very generous with her expertise. It's her time that's usually limited.''

''I was lucky enough to catch her when she had an hour to spare.''

''Yes, you were lucky, weren't you?''

Lydia didn't care for the way the two friends were eyeing each other and talking about her as if she weren't there. She cleared her throat. ''Are you meeting your sister for dinner, Scott?''

''Yes. How did you know?''

She nodded in the direction behind him. ''I see her coming this way from the parking lot.''

Glancing over his shoulder, he greeted his sister. ''Heather. Look who I've found.''

Heather looked speculatively from Lydia to Cameron. ''Well, hello. Did you two have dinner together?''

"Yes, we did," Cameron said with a visible show of patience. "Lydia's helping me with a project."

"How nice." Heather looked genuinely pleased. Probably, Lydia mused, because she had dined with someone other than Heather's brother.

Relieved to have a valid excuse to escape this uncomfortable exchange, Lydia glanced at her watch. "I'd better be going or I'll be late for my class. Heather, Scott, it was nice to see you both again. Cameron, thank you for dinner. I'll get back to you as soon as I've had a chance to look over these papers."

"I'll walk you to your car. See you around, Scott. Good to see you, Heather. Give my regards to your fiancé." Taking Lydia's arm, Cameron nodded to his friends and led her away. Lydia was aware that Scott watched them until his sister urged him inside the restaurant. Cameron whistled beneath his breath as they approached Lydia's car. "Boy, am *I* in hot water."

"Why is that?" she asked, deliberately obtuse.

"You saw the way Scott was scowling at us. He didn't like it at all that we had dinner together."

Lydia shoved her key into her door lock. "That's silly. There's no reason for him to disapprove of our meeting this way."

"No?"

"Of course not. Scott and I have met several times to discuss our work over lunch or dinner. This was no different."

"I'm not sure Scott would agree with you. That was most definitely a no-trespassing look he gave me just now."

She opened her door. "Ridiculous. He and I are just friends. If he says anything to you, you should make it clear there's nothing more between you and me."

"Since you aren't involved with Scott, is there any chance you'd be interested in going out with me? On a real date? Dancing, perhaps, or maybe a symphony performance."

She could hardly believe he'd actually

asked. After a long social drought, it seemed she was suddenly being inundated with invitations from men, two of whom were the type of men who'd rarely paid attention to her before. But there was only one man who seriously tempted her to accept his invitations—and it wasn't Cameron, charming as he was. "Thank you, but no."

She saw no need to elaborate.

Cameron took the rejection well. He acted almost as if he'd expected it. He smiled and helped her into her car. "We'll stick to business, then. I'll talk to you soon, Lydia."

She nodded and closed the door, thinking that maybe she shouldn't be quite so generous with her "expertise" in the future.

"They make a very nice couple."

Scott glared over his menu at his sister. "Don't start, Heather."

"Well, they do," she said, all innocence. "I think someone like Lydia would be very good for Cameron. He's been so rootless and unhappy lately. He needs someone who challenges him.''

''Cameron isn't looking for a mate at the moment, so don't start your matchmaking with him. And especially not with Lydia. Trust me, she and Cam couldn't be more mismatched.''

''I think you're wrong. I have a—''

''Don't start talking about your 'matchmaking instincts,''' he growled, interrupting what he knew was coming. ''Face it, Heather. You aren't that good at it. With the exception of yourself and Steve, you've never successfully matched anyone that I know of.''

She huffed indignantly. ''That's because no one will take my advice. If they'd just listen to me...''

He shook his head and set his menu aside, having little appetite for the dishes he usually enjoyed. The mental picture of Cameron and Lydia walking so cozily out of the restaurant was still plaguing him. The thought of Cameron's hand resting so intimately at Lydia's waist still made his hands want to clench.

Just what was going on anyway? With

them—and with himself? It bothered him a great deal that he was no closer to an answer to the second question than he was to the first.

"I don't know why you're so surly about it," Heather said with a pout. "You're the one who told me you and Lydia are just friends. That's the truth, isn't it?"

Was it? Even Scott couldn't define the relationship that existed between them at the moment. He only knew it was changing—and had been since the first time he kissed her.

"Let's talk about your wedding," he suggested. "Isn't that why we're here?"

She went along cooperatively enough with his change of subject, but he wasn't able to put Lydia out of his mind for the remainder of the evening, no matter how hard he tried.

Lydia wasn't really surprised when Scott called her late that evening.

"How was your class?" he asked.

"Fine. And your dinner with your sister?"

"The food was good, as it always is at Vittorio's. Heather talked all evening about her wedding plans. She asked me to give her away."

"That's very sweet. What did you say?"

"That I would sell her, but I'm not giving her away. I've got too much invested in her to just give her away."

She smiled. "I'm sure you said you would be honored."

"Maybe something like that. So…you had dinner with Cam."

It was a rather inane statement since they both knew she had, but she answered simply, "Yes."

"You're working with him on a story." Again, it wasn't a question.

"You make it sound as if I'm contributing more than I really am. He simply asked me to look over some papers—which I was doing when you called."

"And will you be meeting with him again to discuss your conclusions?"

If she didn't know better, she would swear Scott was acting possessive again. She answered briskly, "Yes, actually. He thought we would need to discuss it in detail. He's taking me to the coast for the weekend so we'll have plenty of time and privacy to, um, talk about his story."

"He's taking you *where?*" Scott nearly shouted the question in her ear.

She sighed loudly. "He's not taking me anywhere, Scott. I'm going to give him a call and let him know what I think about the scientific evidence he's been given for his story. That's it, the total extent of my involvement. Any more questions?"

"You sound a bit annoyed with me," he commented after a brief pause.

"Shouldn't I be? You've interrogated me as if you suspect I'm involved in a crime."

"I'm sorry. It...caught me by surprise to see you leaving the restaurant with Cam tonight. I guess I'm used to thinking of you as my own personal DNA consultant."

Since she didn't know what to say to that, she remained silent.

"Maybe we can get together this weekend

to see that movie?'' he suggested after a moment. ''I'm free Friday evening.''

''I'm afraid I'm not. I've made other plans for Friday evening.''

''Oh. Working again?''

She grimaced. ''Actually, I've made plans with Charlie's friend, Gary.''

After a moment of silence, Scott asked, ''You let Larissa talk you into it?''

''Not exactly. Gary called and asked me to attend a reception at his store, and I couldn't think of a polite way to turn him down.''

''You could have used me for an excuse. You could have told him we're seeing each other.''

''No. I don't like to lie. And maybe the evening will be fun. It can't hurt to give it a try.''

''Then I hope you have a nice time.''

He didn't sound very sincere. ''Thank you,'' she said anyway.

''Well—I guess I'll see you around, then.''

''Yes, of course.''

Lydia hung up the phone a few minutes later with the hollow feeling that whatever had begun to develop between her and Scott was over now. He wasn't a man who would accept rejection well—and she'd repeatedly declined invitations from him since the last evening they'd spent together. He was probably wondering why he'd bothered to ask.

It was a question that had been haunting her since he'd kissed her in her doorway.

He didn't want commitment—he'd said so several times. He had his eye on a partnership and didn't want to even think about a permanent relationship until he obtained it. She understood that. She'd been the same way, zealously guarding her career from anyone who might try to interfere with it.

Lydia and her sister had both learned from their mother's mistakes and her many warnings during their formative years. Violet Hampton had been a premed student in college when she met Clayton McKinley and tumbled recklessly into love with the handsome athlete. A year later, Violet was married and working as a bank teller to put her husband through law school. Clayton had promised to return the favor; as soon as he completed his education, he assured her, she could go to medical school. It was only a two-year delay.

Larissa's accidental conception had postponed the medical school plans. Lydia's birth, followed three years later by Clayton's death in a drunk-driving accident, had put an end to them. There had been an embarrassing scandal when it became widely known that Clayton had been with the young wife of one of the senior partners in his law firm when he died. The affair had apparently been going on for some time. Violet was left alone with two small children, a mountain of debts, a broken heart and a load of shattered dreams.

Too embittered by Clayton's betrayal to ever trust another man, Violet had dedicated the rest of her life to her daughters, encouraging them to pursue their dreams, warning them over and over about those who would try to get in the way.

The sacrifices Lydia made to attain her current position had all been well justified, she thought. She loved her work. She was only months away from her doctorate degree, a goal she'd been working toward for so very long. She'd had nibbles from several prestigious research universities in response to the résumés she'd mailed out. She credited her mother with giving her the drive and confidence to set her goals high and go after them. But had Violet also made Lydia a bit too slow to trust—especially when it came to men?

It had taken Larissa a long time to find someone she trusted with her heart. With her dreams. And Lydia thought her sister had chosen well with Charlie, who would never interfere with Larissa's art career. He was, in fact, her biggest fan and most ardent supporter.

Lydia had begun to question whether she would ever find someone like that for herself.

She wondered what Scott would look for in a mate after he achieved his partnership—as she had no doubt he would do very soon. Would he want a full-time wife? Someone to make a home for him and his children, to entertain his clients and represent him well at the country club and in the community? Someone whose only purpose was to make him happy? According to Violet, that was the kind of wife Clayton had wanted. And she had nearly destroyed herself trying to be that for him.

Lydia knew she would never be anyone's "little woman." Her work would always be too important to her for her to ever be able to walk away from it. She would like to think she could make time for a family; she knew other women who successfully juggled the demands of work and family, though she knew it wasn't easy. Her own mother had managed to support her children while working her way to a vice presidency of the bank. It wasn't the medical career Violet had dreamed of, but it seemed to give her some fulfillment. When she was diagnosed with late-stage ovarian cancer, she'd admitted that she'd neglected her annual checkups because she didn't like taking time away from work.

Lydia had learned from that lesson, too. She'd guarded her health as faithfully as she'd protected her career.

She was guarding her heart now by avoiding

an entanglement with Scott, she assured herself. She knew herself well enough to recognize that he posed the greatest danger to her emotional well-being since Kenny had hurt her so badly during graduate school.

She didn't want to be hurt again. And it seemed to her that the safest measure was to make sure she and Scott never ventured again beyond the comfortable boundaries of friendship.

Chapter Eight

Gary Dunston had offered to pick Lydia up for the bookstore event Friday evening, but she had declined the offer, telling him she would meet him there. Already regretting the impulse that made her accept his invitation, she wished she had come up with an excuse and stayed home with a good book instead. She had a nagging suspicion that she'd accepted Gary's invitation as a reaction to her real desire to spend more time with Scott. She wasn't proud of herself if that was her real motivation.

That vague sense of guilt gave her extra patience during the less-than-successful evening. Ten people, including Lydia, Gary and the author, showed up for the reception and book signing. As far as Lydia could tell, the other seven were there for the free food. Considering that the snacks consisted of dry cheese on Ritz crackers, chocolate chip cookies poured from a bag onto a paper plate, and Hawaiian Punch served in paper cups, Lydia wasn't sure it was really worth their effort.

The author signed two books. One of them for Gary. He spent the next hour and a half trying to convince Lydia that bacteria were sentient beings trying to establish an intelligent dialogue with their host bodies. Not even for the sake of courtesy could Lydia bring herself to spend her money on one of the inexpensively bound volumes in which he expounded on that ludicrous theory.

She turned to Gary in disbelief after he'd seen the author and the last food freeloader out of the store. "How on earth did that man convince anyone to actually publish that garbage?"

Gary cleared his throat. "Actually, he self-published. I agreed to carry a few copies in my inventory because I find his ideas interesting, if improbable."

"Improbable? Gary, the man believes that he can communicate with bacteria! He thinks they're controlling our actions through thought transfer. He's a fruitcake."

"It *would* make an interesting science fiction premise," Gary said weakly.

"But he doesn't think he's writing fiction of any type. He seems to believe his theories. He said all diseases could be cured if we would just make friends with the microorganisms that cause them!"

"So you didn't enjoy the evening?" Gary looked crestfallen, his round face drooping.

Now she felt guilty for speaking her mind. Guilt seemed to be her most common reaction to this man, she thought ruefully.

"It was a very interesting evening," she assured her host, trying to make amends. "I didn't agree with anything the man said, but

I've certainly never met anyone else quite like him.''

Apparently cheered by her careful comments, Gary smiled again. ''I have a nice bottle of wine in my apartment upstairs, and some better snacks than I served those moochers tonight. Would you like to sit with me for a while? We could talk about your work—the scientific, rather than science fiction, study of microbes.''

Guilt could only push her so far. ''Thank you, Gary, but not tonight. I've put in a full day and have to get an early start in the morning. I really need to get some rest.''

His expressive face immediately drooped again. ''Yes, of course. Um…the man who accompanied you to your sister's party? Are you and he…?''

Now was her chance, Lydia thought, to use Scott as a convenient excuse. He'd even volunteered to serve. But she still couldn't do it. ''Scott and I are friends and neighbors.''

The spark of hope in Gary's pale brown eyes made her wonder if honesty had been the right choice. If he had any real interest in her—and she'd done nothing to deliberately pique his interest—she certainly didn't want to encourage him. "Some other time, then?" he suggested.

"Perhaps." She kept her reply deliberately vague and unencouraging—the most she could do short of an outright refusal.

He seemed to be satisfied. Nodding energetically, making his curly mop of hair flop onto his forehead, he walked her to the door. "Are you sure there's no book you would like to take with you? My treat."

It wasn't the first time that evening he'd made the offer. Lydia declined, as she had the other times. "I really don't have time to read for pleasure during the next few weeks. I have too much required reading to get through by the end of the school term."

"If there's ever anything I can provide for you, don't hesitate to ask. I can obtain almost any book title you could possibly want."

So could she, either through the university library or over the Internet. But she merely murmured, ‘‘I’ll keep that in mind. Thank you.’’

‘‘I’ll walk you to your car.’’

‘‘No need. I’m parked right outside your door.’’ It wasn’t as if the small parking lot had been crowded.

‘‘Okay, then. Good night, Lydia. Thank you for coming. We’ll see each other again soon.’’

She nodded noncommittally and slipped out the door.

What had made her think she needed a social life? she asked herself as she slid gratefully behind the wheel of her car. She’d been doing perfectly well without one until now.

It was a week later before Lydia saw Scott again. As happened occasionally, they both turned into the apartment complex parking lot at the same time. Determined to behave toward him exactly as she had before they attempted their dating-for-convenience plan, she smiled pleasantly. ‘‘Hello, Scott.’’

Tucking his briefcase beneath his arm, Scott approached her. He was smiling, she noted, but the smile wasn't reflected in his dark green eyes. He looked tired. Maybe a little pale. And his voice was a bit gravelly when he said, "Hi, Lydia. How are you?"

"*I'm* fine. I'm not so sure you can say the same. Are you ill?"

"No. I'm fine," he assured her, and then coughed.

"You're coming down with something, aren't you?"

He shook his head. "I never get sick."

"You have a peace treaty with your bacteria, I suppose?" she asked dryly.

"I beg your pardon?"

"I'll tell you about it sometime." She glanced up at the low gray clouds above them. "It looks as if it's about to rain."

"You'd better get inside, then. It's good to see you, Lydia."

He wasn't smiling when he said it. Nor was she when she answered. "It's good to see you, too."

She turned and hurried to her apartment before she revealed just how good it felt to see him after so many days of thinking about him.

She couldn't stop thinking about Scott that evening and she woke up thinking about him Saturday morning. She kept picturing the way he'd looked in the parking lot, his skin pale, his eyes overly bright, his voice hoarse. He had definitely been ill, even if his male pride kept him from admitting it. She wondered if he was feeling better this morning. She wondered if he would call anyone if he wasn't.

She debated calling him. She actually put her hand on the phone several times, then talked herself out of it each time. Until finally she couldn't stand it any longer and dialed his number before she could change her mind again. She hardly recognized his voice when he answered.

"You're feeling worse, aren't you?" she asked.

"Well..."

"Have you taken anything for your symptoms? Do you have any fruit juice?"

"No, I..." He paused as if it hurt him to talk. "I feel pretty rotten," he finally admitted.

"I'm coming down to check on you. Unless you'd rather I call your sister?"

"No!" he croaked. "For God's sake, don't call Heather."

"Then I'll come down. Do you have any juice? Any over-the-counter medications?"

"I...uh...not sure."

"Never mind. Just unlock the door for me. I'll be there shortly."

She hung up with a shake of her head, thinking that she'd never met a man who handled illness well no matter how capable he might be in every other aspect of his life.

Scott looked miserable when he opened his door wearing only a pair of drawstring-waist khaki shorts. His eyes were red and swollen, his cheeks flushed with fever, his jaw unshaven, his hair disheveled. So why did she still find him so disconcertingly attractive?

She hid the familiar reaction to him behind a brusque tone as she stepped past him, keeping her eyes averted from his bare chest. The brief glance she'd managed had been enough to assure her that he'd been hiding a spectacular body beneath his clothes.

"I brought a few things I thought you might need," she said, indicating the shopping bag she was carrying. "Have you taken anything for your fever?"

"No. How do you know I even have a fever?"

"I can tell by looking at you." To confirm her assessment, she laid a hand against his whisker-rough cheek. "Oh, yes, you definitely have a fever. And you're swaying on your feet. Go back to bed, Scott. I'll bring you some juice and medicine. Do you have any symptoms other than the fever and sore throat?"

"My head hurts. And I can't breathe through my nose," he complained. "But I'm not sick."

"Of course not," she replied with a roll of her eyes. "But you should still go back to bed."

It was a measure of exactly how badly he

did feel that he went without further argument, his steps unsteady.

Shaking her head again, Lydia carried her bag of supplies into the kitchen. Scott apparently had not eaten anything that morning. There were no dirty dishes, only a couple of used drinking glasses. She rinsed them and placed them in the empty dishwasher, then assembled a tray with a glass of orange juice, a pastry she'd brought with her and two acetaminophen tablets.

Scott was lying facedown on his bed on top of the covers, as if he'd barely managed to make it that far before collapsing. Setting the tray on the nightstand, she reached out to help him get settled more comfortably on his back against the pillows. It took all the objectivity she could muster to keep her thoughts away from how good his warm skin felt beneath her hands, how intimate this situation was, just the two of them alone in his bedroom.

He sneezed loudly, drawing her out of her daydreaming.

"Take these," she said, holding the tablets

to his lips along with the glass of juice. As cooperative as a child, Scott swallowed the tablets with some difficulty, groaning when his sore throat protested. "Try to drink the rest of the juice," she urged him, steadying the glass for him. "You need to keep up your strength. Do you think you can eat a little something?"

"Not hungry," he said, but he managed to finish most of the juice.

"Do you have a thermometer?"

"No. I never get sick."

He should have figured out by now that the power of positive thinking didn't always work. He could deny it as much as he wanted, but he was still sick.

"Maybe you're just tired," she said to placate him. "Get some sleep, Scott. I'll check on you later."

"No, I have things to do. I need to..." His eyes closed. A minute later, he was asleep.

Lydia hovered beside the bed for a few minutes, watching him with a worried frown. She wondered if he had any appointments she should cancel for him. If there was anyone she should call. He'd seemed very opposed to her calling his sister, but was there anyone else?

Seeing how soundly he was sleeping, she decided not to disturb him to ask. The world could get along without Scott Pearson for one Saturday morning, she thought. He needed to rest.

Scott had no idea what time it was when he surfaced. He had to almost pry his eyes open, and his vision was blurry when he did. His head pounded and his mouth was cottony. Every inch of his body ached.

Maybe he would just go back to sleep, he thought, closing his eyes again. Then forced them back open when a hazy memory surfaced in his fever-dulled mind. Had Lydia actually been in his bedroom earlier? Had she tucked him into bed and given him orange juice and pills? Or had he only been dreaming?

He looked around the bedroom but saw no evidence of her. His apartment was quiet. If she had been there, she was gone now.

He was so thirsty. And his head felt as if it

might explode at any minute. Maybe some more juice and medicine would help. Groaning, he rolled out of bed, feeling as if he'd aged a couple of decades while he slept. The floor seemed to shift beneath his bare feet when he stood. He swayed, then clutched the dresser to steady himself.

He could do this, he told himself, focusing grimly on the bedroom doorway—which seemed to be moving farther away from him even as he stared at it. All he had to do was put one foot in front of the other....

He lurched forward, bruising his hip on the corner of the dresser, bumping his shoulder against the doorjamb. But he made it into the hallway, where he propped one hand against the wall and walked slowly to the living room.

He paused in the doorway, staring at the couch, where Lydia sat with a notebook computer open in her lap and several neat piles of papers stacked around her. Her sister's painting, which had been delivered only a few days earlier, hung on the wall behind her. Scott had thought the painting added elegance to his living room. But that had been before he'd seen Lydia here and understood what true beauty was.

She looked up, her gaze locking with his, then set the computer aside and rose quickly to her feet. "What are you doing out of bed?" she scolded, hurrying toward him. "You look as though you're about to fall flat on your face."

"You're here," he said stupidly.

"I didn't want to leave you alone. Do you feel any better?"

Holding himself upright through sheer force of will, he lifted one shoulder. "I'm fine."

She wrinkled her nose at him. "You're a liar."

"Yeah," he admitted, feeling sheepish. "I feel lousy."

"I thought so." She took his arm. "Come on. Let's get you back into bed."

"If you only knew how long I've been waiting to hear you say that," he murmured with a weak attempt at humor.

"Behave yourself. You're in no condition to be making passes."

He allowed her to help him lower himself to the bed. "You're beautiful when you're bossy."

"Be quiet and lie down. Where were you going just now?"

He settled gratefully back against the pillows, trying to hide his shakiness. "The kitchen."

"Are you hungry?"

"No. Thirsty. And my head's killing me."

"I'll get you something. Don't move until I come back."

That sounded like a very good idea to him since every movement set off another round of explosions in his head. He closed his eyes and lay very still.

Maybe he drifted off again. It seemed that no time at all had passed before she was back, holding a pill to his lips. "Can you swallow this?" she asked, her voice gentle.

The small tablet felt like a boulder when it passed through his sore throat, but he managed to wash it down with a few sips of juice. And then he swallowed the second pill she gave him, finishing the juice afterward.

"I called my doctor," Lydia told him, setting the empty glass on the nightstand. "She said you probably have the flu. Apparently, there's a lot of it going around. She said you should rest, monitor your fever, drink plenty of fluids and treat your symptoms with over-the-counter medications. If you become significantly worse, she suggested you contact your own doctor, but you'll probably just have to suffer through it. She said you would feel better in a week or so."

"A week?" He shook his head, then pressed his fingertips to his throbbing temples. "I can't be sick for a week. I don't have time."

"I'm not sure it's up to you at this point," she answered with sympathetic humor. "Face it, Scott. You're sick."

He groaned and dropped his head back into the pillows. "Damn."

"Do you need me to make any calls for

you? Are you sure you don't want me to call your sister?''

He nearly shuddered. ''Please, no. I adore my sister, Lydia, but I can't deal with her when I'm flat on my back.''

''Anyone else, then?''

''No. I don't have any firm obligations until Monday morning. I'm sure I'll be up and around by then.''

''We'll see.'' He noted that she didn't sound so confident. ''In the meantime,'' she went on, ''try to get some more rest. It's the best thing for you. When you wake up again, I'll have some soup or broth ready for you. Maybe you'll be hungry then.''

''Thanks.'' The thought of food still didn't appeal to him, but maybe it would later. ''Lydia?''

With one last pat to his pillow, she straightened. ''Yes?''

''Don't you have other things you should be doing?''

''Nothing I can't do here,'' she assured him.

"Actually, this is giving me a chance to get a lot done and still keep an eye on you."

"You're being very kind."

She brushed a limp strand of hair away from his damp forehead. "This is what friends do, Scott. They help each other."

He closed his eyes, deciding to think about that later. For some reason, his brain didn't seem to be working right. He only knew that it felt damn good to have Lydia's cool hand stroking his forehead as he drifted off to sleep.

Scott's phone rang several times during the afternoon. Lydia turned down the ringer and let his machine pick up. She made a couple of trips up to her own apartment to check messages and retrieve things she needed, but she didn't stay away very long. She didn't like leaving Scott alone when he was so sick.

Twice she tiptoed into his bedroom to check on him. He slept soundly, a faint crease between his eyebrows indicating that even in sleep he was uncomfortable. She lingered by his bed a bit longer than absolutely necessary.

She wasn't really ogling his bare chest, she assured herself, though she couldn't help but notice how good he looked against his sheets. She just wanted to make sure he was okay.

Yeah, right, she thought, forcing herself to walk away. Even she didn't believe that one.

She was able to accomplish quite a lot of work that day, uninterrupted since no one knew where she was. Scott woke several times and seemed to feel worse as the day passed. The doctor had warned her that he would feel worse before he got better, so she was prepared even though she felt sorry for him. He was thoroughly frustrated by his inability to shake off his illness and get right back to his usual routines.

He seemed to take her presence almost for granted, meekly submitting to her instructions when she forced medicines and liquids into him. She thought his acquiescence was probably a measure of how sick he was. He didn't even feel well enough to question her right to walk into his apartment and take over.

The only time he balked was when she tried

to get him to eat. Just the thought of food made him nauseous, he insisted. He would take only juice. As long as he was drinking liquids, she was satisfied.

It was after 6:00 p.m. before he woke enough for a coherent conversation again. She had just given him a fever reducer and a glass of cool water. His eyes were unusually bright, she noted, and there were dark patches of color high on his cheeks. The thermometer she'd brought down from her apartment read 102. She was sure he felt truly awful. "Would you like a cool cloth for your head?"

"No. I'm fine."

He seemed so determined to insist that he was okay. She nodded and sat on the very edge of the bed. "I'm glad to hear that. Want to go out for a run?"

He gave her a weak smile. "Okay, maybe I'm not that fine."

"I didn't think so. Why is it so hard for you to admit that you're sick?"

"I don't know." He grimaced. "I guess I'm just used to being the one who takes care of everyone else, not the one who needs to be taken care of.''

''You must have been the man of your family for a long time,'' she guessed.

''My father died in an accident when Heather and I were twelve. Mom was one of those dependent, sort of clingy types who never even paid a bill or changed a lightbulb for herself before she was widowed. I kind of got in the habit of taking care of things for her while she was alive.''

''And you've watched out for your sister ever since your mother died, even though she considers herself the older sibling.''

''Heather takes care of herself on the whole.''

Lydia was sure Heather did take care of herself physically, but from what she had observed, Scott gave his sister a lot of emotional support. It was no wonder he hated being dependent even for this short time and in such a small way. He had no prior experience at it.

Scott cleared his throat, trying to ease some

of the hoarseness. ''Tell me about your family, Lydia.''

She wondered why he asked. ''What about them?''

He shifted against the pillow, the movement restless. ''Talking helps me keep my mind off my aches and pains. Unless you have other things you need to do?''

If conversation made him feel better, she would certainly chat with him for a while. But she wasn't sure how to begin. ''My father was an attorney.''

His eyebrows rose in surprise. ''You never mentioned that before.''

''He died when I was three. I don't even remember him.''

''Does Larissa's antipathy toward attorneys have anything to do with your father?''

''Probably. He died while driving drunk with his mistress.''

Scott winced. ''I'm sorry.''

She shrugged, wondering why she'd been quite so candid. ''As I said, I don't even re-member him. And I've always thought Larissa was wrong to hold our father's behavior against an entire profession.''

''What was your mother like?''

''The opposite of yours, apparently. She was the one who worked to put her husband through school and helped him establish his career rather than allow herself to be cared for. Instead of encouraging us to be dependent on men, she constantly warned us not to let men hold us back from what we really wanted to do. She made a lot of personal sacrifices for her marriage, and my father's behavior didn't exactly reward her for what she gave up for him.''

Scott nodded thoughtfully, his bleary eyes focused on Lydia's face. ''And because of your parents' mistakes, you've decided to remain single?''

''I didn't say that. I'm not opposed to marriage or children, but I've concentrated first on getting my career established. I've always believed a woman should be able to support herself. I happened to pursue a career that takes several years to train for.''

"I have friends—men and women—who married young and still pursued demanding careers. Doctors, attorneys, educators—people who found spouses who supported them in their goals rather than holding them back."

"I'm sure there are many couples like that," she agreed. "However, the few men I've been involved with during the past few years became very impatient when my busy schedule conflicted with their interests."

"Sounds to me," he murmured, his eyelids growing heavy again, "as if you've dated the wrong men."

"Obviously." She tucked the bedcovers more snugly around him. "And have you stayed single because you didn't want a dependent woman like your mother—or because you *do?*"

His faint smile was lopsided. "I don't think I know. Clingy, dependent women don't interest me. And yet, when I fell head over heels while I was in law school, I was crushed when the woman I loved chose her career over me. She wanted to be a network news anchor—and she decided she needed to be completely unattached to get there. Since then, it seemed easier not to put anyone in the position of having to choose.''

She thought of the relationship he'd apparently had with Paula—no commitment, no expectations, no deep feelings to be crushed when it ended. She could understand the attraction in such a relationship, but she wasn't sure she could stay objective enough to make it work. She had never been able to separate physical from emotional intimacy—she doubted that she would ever be able to do so with Scott.

Even now, sitting at his bedside as he lay ill, she was flooded with feelings for him. Sympathy, certainly. A desire to alleviate his discomfort. If there was more, she didn't want to analyze it just then.

His eyes were almost closed now, his voice slurred. ``Lydia?''

``Yes?''

``Thank you for all you've done for me today.''

"You're welcome. Go to sleep now. Perhaps you'll feel better when you wake up."

"I'd have to feel better to die," he muttered.

"Men are always such babies when they're sick," she teased, lightly patting his overly warm cheek as she rose. "Good night, Scott."

He murmured something she didn't understand, then slid quietly into sleep. Lydia stood over him for a few minutes longer, fighting a foolish urge to lean over and kiss his forehead. Telling herself to stop being an idiot, she turned and left the bedroom.

She couldn't decide what to do then. She'd eaten a sandwich for dinner and finished most of the work she'd brought down with her. She supposed she really should leave for the night. She could always come back early in the morning to check on him.

But what if his fever shot up during the night? She'd seen how weak and dizzy he was; what if he fell on the way to the bathroom and hit his head? She couldn't bear the thought of leaving him sick and alone all night even though she knew he was perfectly capable of taking care of himself.

Maybe she would just hang around a little while longer, she decided. Just to make sure Scott was all right.

Chapter Nine

It was a good thing, Lydia concluded near dawn, that she had decided to stay. Scott had had a dreadful night. She would have hated to think of him going through that alone.

His fever spiked twice, hitting 104 degrees. The high temperature made him achy and miserable, nearly unresponsive when she tried to talk to him. She worried about convulsions and delirium, and fretted about dehydration, but she was able to control the fever through medication and cold compresses. He didn't want water, but she forced several ounces into him during the night. She replaced his hot, wrinkled pillowcases with fresh, cool ones, steadied him with a supportive shoulder when he made his way to the bathroom, then hovered outside the door to help him back to bed when he finished.

When she slept, it was in snatches on his couch, but even then she only dozed, ready to act upon any sound from the bedroom.

It was a long, difficult night, but Lydia didn't regret her decision to stay. She believed Scott would have done as much for her if she'd needed him—though the idea of being so vulnerable in front of him was oddly disconcerting.

Exhaustion claimed her near dawn, and she fell more heavily into sleep than before. She didn't stir until she felt someone touch her. She woke then with a start.

Scott was leaning over her, his expression apologetic. "I'm sorry. I was trying to cover you with this afghan. I thought you might be cold."

She pushed a hand through her tangled hair,

aware of how wrinkled and disheveled she must look after a near sleepless night in her clothes. Not that Scott looked any better, she observed, studying his bloodshot eyes and two-day growth of beard.

Still holding the knitted afghan, he stepped back as she sat up. "How do you feel?" she asked.

"Like I've been run over by a stampede of elephants," he admitted, sinking to sit beside her on the couch as if he wasn't sure his legs would support him any longer.

She lifted a hand to his forehead. "Your fever is up again. But not as high as it was during the night, thank goodness."

He grimaced, looking self-conscious. "Bad night, wasn't it?"

"You were very ill. I was really worried at times. I came very close to taking you to the hospital at one point, but you refused to even consider it. Do you remember?"

"Vaguely. But as you can see, I was right. I didn't need to go to the hospital."

"If your fever had climbed one more degree, you'd have gone if I had to carry you out over my shoulder."

"It might have been amusing to watch you try that stunt," he said with a shadow of his usual cocky grin.

"Don't think I wouldn't have if I'd thought it necessary."

"I'm learning never to underestimate you, Lydia."

Something in his gruff voice made her flush and glance away. "It's been four hours since you took anything for fever," she said with a quick glance at her watch. "Do you think you could eat a muffin or some fruit? Or oatmeal would go down easily—do you like oatmeal?"

She was babbling—suddenly oddly conscious of being alone with him, both of them sleep tousled, Scott still bare-chested and heavy-lidded. During the night, she had been too busy and too worried to give any thought to their complex relationship—the attraction that simmered between them, the kisses that kept haunting her, the casual friendship that had turned into something more precarious.

Now she wondered just what she was doing here.

"I like oatmeal." Scott watched her as if he was wondering what she was thinking. "But I don't expect you to cook for me."

Still avoiding his eyes, she shrugged. "Actually, I'm hungry, too. I'll make oatmeal for both of us. But first, I'd like to freshen up."

He ran a hand over his jaw. "I could stand a shower and a shave myself."

"Will you be all right while I run upstairs for a few minutes?" She eyed him doubtfully. "You're still weak and feverish. Not very steady. Maybe you should wait until I come back down to take your shower, just in case there's a problem."

His smile suddenly strengthened, making him look more like his usual slick, confident self. "Are you offering to give me a bath, Lydia?"

She rose to her feet and gave him a warning glare. "I'm tired, grubby and grouchy, Pearson. Don't push your luck."

He laughed. ''Have I ever told you how much I genuinely like you, Lydia McKinley?''

Completely disarmed, she cleared her throat. ''I'll be back soon,'' she said, turning abruptly toward the door. ''Don't try to do too much until I return.''

Twenty minutes later, she had showered and dressed in clean clothes, her wet hair held away from her face with clips, only a minimum of makeup hiding the traces of her difficult night. She had needed that time away from Scott if only to recover from the effects of having him look at her so warmly and tell her that he liked her.

The simple words shouldn't have meant so much to her, she thought in despair. They were hardly a declaration of undying devotion. But the rich sincerity in his voice had warmed her all the way to her heart.

Careful, McKinley, she warned herself as she set breakfast supplies in a basket to carry downstairs. *Be very careful.*

Scott was asleep again, lying on his side on the bed. He'd showered and shaved, she noticed. His hair was still damp. He wore a white V-neck T-shirt and a pair of navy drawstring shorts. He'd apparently used all his strength to clean up and dress.

She considered letting him sleep, but she thought he needed to eat. And she had forgotten to give him his fever medication before she left, probably because he'd rattled her with his comments.

"Scott?" When he didn't immediately respond to her voice, she laid a hand lightly on his shoulder. "Scott?"

He opened his eyes, blinked, then rolled onto his back and captured her hand with his. "You weren't gone long."

"More than half an hour. You've been sleeping."

"You look nice."

Since her own hair was still damp and she wore nothing more fancy than a plain yellow sweater and dark jeans, she attributed his compliment to fever. "Thank you," she said briskly. "I have your breakfast ready. Will you try to eat something?"

He didn't look very enthusiastic about the prospect, but he nodded. "I'll try."

She pulled her hand from his, then rested it on his forehead. Still too warm, she noted. "Have you taken anything since I left?"

"No."

"The medicine's in the kitchen. You can have that for an appetizer."

"Yum."

She smiled. "Try to control your enthusiasm."

He sighed and pushed himself upright. With her help, he rose, then swayed. She wrapped an arm around his waist, steadying him.

"I really don't like this," Scott muttered, lifting his free hand to his forehead. "I hate feeling so out of control."

"I know. Overachievers like us hate to be sick. Hate having to admit that no amount of hard work or determination will hurry the process along until the illness has run its course. It's against everything we believe in to delegate so much responsibility to our immune systems."

His arm tightened around her shoulders as they made their way slowly toward the kitchen. ‘‘I suppose you’re right. My immune system isn’t responding well to my orders. That always ticks me off.’’

He needed her assistance, she reminded herself, staying close to him. There was nothing really personal about walking arm in arm with him through his apartment. And there was absolutely no reason she shouldn’t enjoy the interlude while it lasted, she added, allowing herself to notice how strong and solid he felt against her.

Seated at his kitchen table, Scott gulped down his pills, then toyed with his oatmeal.

‘‘Eat,’’ Lydia ordered after spooning up some of her own.

He obligingly took a small bite, swallowed, then just twisted his spoon in the bowl again.

Watching him, Lydia sighed. ‘‘I know you don’t feel hungry, Scott, but you really should try to eat a little more.’’

He took a few more spoonfuls and finished

his juice, then pushed the bowl away. "I can't eat any more."

She nodded, satisfied that he'd had enough to suffice for now. She would try to get some soup into him at lunchtime, she decided, already accepting that she would be spending another day taking care of him. As long as he was running a fever, she wouldn't feel comfortable leaving him alone.

He wouldn't go back to bed after breakfast, saying that he was thoroughly tired of the sight of his bedroom ceiling. He settled instead on the couch, starting out upright, but gradually shifting until he was stretched out with his head on a throw pillow, his bare feet crossed on the opposite arm of the couch. Lydia turned on the television and handed him the remote, then curled up in a big armchair with a stack of essay exams she had to grade by the next day. She kicked off her shoes and tucked her feet beneath her, a diet soda on the end table beside her.

"Are you comfortable?" Scott asked, glancing away from the ball game on TV.

"Quite, thank you. Is there anything I can get for you?"

"No, I'm fine. I should probably try to talk you into going back to your apartment, but I'm afraid I'm too selfish. I like having you here with me."

She smiled. "I'm doing here exactly what I would be doing in my own apartment. You aren't keeping me from anything."

"Good. But if there *is* anything you need to do, feel free. I'll be okay on my own."

Brave words, she thought, from a guy who couldn't even stand up without assistance. "I'll keep that in mind."

He turned his attention back to the ball game and she looked back down at her work. A few minutes later, she glanced up again and smiled. She doubted that Scott was following the game very closely with his eyes closed. He had fallen asleep again, his lips parted, his breathing a bit labored, but not enough to cause her concern. The cold-and-flu medication he'd taken earlier was probably making him drowsy but seemed to be alleviating some of his symptoms.

She shifted into a more comfortable position, took a sip of her soda and went back to work.

Scott had a little soup for lunch, but not as much as Lydia would have liked. He was feeling worse again, she could tell. Remembering her doctor's prediction that the illness would progress this way, Lydia tried her best to keep him hydrated and as comfortable as possible. By late afternoon, he was resting a bit more easily again, in his bed this time. She went back to grading, the television tuned to an old movie. She was almost finished with her work when the doorbell rang.

After hesitating a moment, she stood and crossed the room, wondering if Scott had been expecting anyone. She doubted it would be a delivery this late on a Sunday afternoon. When she checked the security viewer and recognized the woman on the other side of Scott's door, she knew she was going to be interrogated.

She opened the door. ''Hello, Heather.''

Scott's sister frowned in surprise, studying Lydia in silence for a moment. Lydia was well aware that she looked as if she'd been making herself at home. She had forgotten to put her shoes on before answering the door. ''Hello, Lydia. This is a surprise.''

She was sure it was. She noted that Heather didn't call it a ''nice'' surprise. ''Come in,'' she said, moving out of the doorway to allow Scott's sister to enter.

''Thank you.'' Her tone a bit stiff, she walked in, a large envelope clutched in her arms. ''Where's Scott? I've been trying to call him all weekend, but he hasn't returned my calls. I, um, guess he's been busy.''

''He's been ill, actually,'' Lydia answered. ''Scott has the flu.''

''Scott's ill?'' Heather's eyes widened. ''Where is he? Is he okay? Why wasn't I called?''

''He's in bed, sleeping. He feels pretty rotten, but he seems to be a little better.'' Lydia didn't answer Heather's final question. No way was she going to divulge that Scott had ordered her not to call his twin.

Heather was already moving toward Scott's bedroom. Lydia hesitated, then followed, uncertain whether she should but feeling compelled to do so. She paused in the doorway.

Heather bustled straight across Scott's bedroom and put her hand on his forehead. "Oh, my goodness, he's burning up with fever! Scott? Can you hear me?"

Abruptly awakened from his deep, medicated sleep, Scott opened his eyes and blinked up at her. "Heather?" Her name was a groggy croak.

"Yes, I'm here. Why didn't you call me? I could have been taking care of you. You're so pale and hot. I'll call Steve and ask him to come straight over."

"No." He put a hand to his head, looking as if he was trying to clear his thoughts. "Don't call Steve. Where's Lydia?"

"I'm here," Lydia said from the doorway. "Is there something I can get for you?"

He shook his head. "Just checking. Did you call Heather?"

"No, she did not." Heather sounded indignant. "I still wouldn't know you were sick if I hadn't just happened to stop by with those Christmas photos I promised to bring you."

"I asked Lydia not to call you. I knew you were busy with wedding plans this weekend. There was no need for you to be concerned."

"Scott, of *course* I'm concerned. Wouldn't you want to know if *I* was sick? And I'm engaged to a doctor, for heaven's sake. He could have been treating you."

Lydia had actually forgotten that Heather's fiancé was a doctor. She wondered guiltily if she should have ignored Scott's instructions and called Heather when she first realized Scott was ill.

"Lydia called her own doctor," Scott said. "She found out what to watch out for. I've been in good hands, Heather."

Heather flicked a look at Lydia. "That's good to hear," she murmured, her expression closed. "Lydia, if you need a break, I can stay with my brother for a while. I'm sure you have plans of your own.''

Lydia couldn't quite interpret the look Scott gave her, but she thought he was asking her not to go. ''Actually, I don't have other plans,'' she said. ''I was just going to make something for Scott's dinner.''

''I can do that.''

''Don't you have a dinner party to attend with Steve tonight?'' Scott asked.

''Yes, I do,'' Heather answered reluctantly. ''But if you need me, I can—''

''No.'' Scott pushed himself upright. Lydia could only guess at the effort he must have made to sit up straight and smile reassuringly at his sister. ''I'm feeling a lot better. There's really no need for you to stay. Lydia's right upstairs if I need anything, and I promise I'll have her call you and Steve if anything changes.''

''Well...'' Heather vacillated, wringing her hands. ''You're sure? You still feel awfully warm.''

''That's only because I've been sleeping,''

he assured her. ''I'm almost back to normal, actually. Another couple of pills and another night's sleep and I'll be as good as new. Don't miss your dinner party.''

''Well, all right. But call me later and let me know how you're doing, okay? Or at least answer your phone so I can talk to you.''

''I'll keep in touch,'' he promised.

''I guess I'd better go, then. Walk me out, Lydia?''

Hiding her surprise, Lydia nodded. ''Of course.''

She and Scott exchanged glances—Scott's rather apologetic—and then Lydia turned to escort Heather to the front door.

''I want to tell Steve about Scott's symptoms,'' Heather said, turning to Lydia in the living room. ''How long has he been ill?''

''He started feeling badly on Friday. He finally admitted he was sick sometime yesterday.''

''Fever? Sore throat? Headache?''

''All of the above, as well as muscle aches

Classic flu symptoms, according to my doctor.''

''So...'' Heather's tone suddenly turned suspiciously casual. ''You've been here all weekend?''

''Yes. I didn't want to leave Scott alone while he was running a fever. I was able to get some work done while he slept,'' she added, motioning toward the paperwork still stacked by her chair.

''It was very kind of you to take care of him this way.'' Heather eyed Lydia assessingly.

Keeping her expression unrevealing, Lydia replied, ''It seemed like the neighborly thing to do.''

''I do wish you'd called me, though.''

Heather was obviously feeling threatened again. Lydia spoke reassuringly. ''Scott didn't want to worry you. And I think he just hated to admit he was ill. He wouldn't have even told me if I hadn't happened to notice when I ran into him in the parking lot. I sort of insisted that he let me take care of him since he wouldn't ask anyone else for help.''

Thoughtful now, Heather nodded. ‘‘He’s never liked admitting when he was sick—not that he is very often. And he hates being hovered over—which I suppose I would have done.’’

Lydia kept quiet.

‘‘Okay, well, I’d better go. You’ll call if he needs me? Steve and I can be here very quickly if he gets worse.’’

‘‘I’ll call.’’

With another last look toward Scott’s bedroom, Heather moved reluctantly to the door.

Lydia waited until Heather was gone, then walked back into Scott’s bedroom. He was lying on his back, one arm draped over his eyes.

‘‘Are you really feeling much better,’’ she asked, ‘‘or were you putting on a show for your sister?’’

He spoke without moving. ‘‘A show. Definitely a show.’’

‘‘You’re not feeling any better?’’

‘‘Just remember when I’m dead that everything I own goes to Heather. Except for my college bowling trophy. You can have that for taking such good care of me.''

She chuckled. ''What? I don't get the sports car?''

''Sorry. The bank gets that. I still owe forty-six payments.''

She laughed softly, pleased that he was at least feeling well enough to make a few bad jokes. ''I'm going to start dinner. Could you eat some grilled chicken? A little rice, maybe?''

He lifted his arm to peer blearily at her. ''Instead of rice, could you make mashed potatoes? My mom always made mashed potatoes for me when I was sick as a kid.''

''You've got it.''

He gave her a weak smile. ''You can have my bowling trophy *and* my bowling shoes.''

''Oh, stop. You'll spoil me.'' She moved toward the door. ''I'll let you know when dinner is ready.''

''If I live that long.''

''Don't be such a wuss,'' she said over her shoulder.

He sighed contentedly. ''I'm really glad you're here, Lydia. Heather would be driving me crazy babying me.''

She couldn't come up with an answer, so she merely nodded and headed for the kitchen.

Because he was expecting Heather to check on him frequently, Scott answered the phone when it rang a half hour later. ''H'lo?''

''Hey. Were you asleep? You sound hoarse.''

Recognizing Cameron's voice, Scott explained, ''I've got the flu.''

''You feel like you've been run over by a truck? Like you really want to die, but it just seems like too much trouble?''

Scott chuckled gruffly. ''Something along that line.''

''Sounds like the flu all right. Remember when I had it last year? I never felt so lousy in my life.''

Scott could identify with that. Last night had been hell. He hated to think how much worse it would have been if Lydia hadn't been there.

"So, you need anything?" Cameron asked a bit awkwardly. "I could come by and...I don't know...sit with you or something."

"Would you rub my toes and read me bedtime stories?" Scott quipped because the offer had rather touched him.

"No. But I might dump a pitcher of cool water over your poor, feverish head," Cameron retorted.

"As much as I appreciate the offer, it isn't necessary. I have help."

"Heather and her fiancé are taking care of you, I suppose. Pretty convenient having a doctor in the family, hmm?"

"Heather stopped by earlier," Scott said. Then added with a touch of smugness, "But Lydia has been watching out for me all weekend."

It was probably less than noble of him to make sure Cameron knew where Lydia had spent the weekend. Scott wasn't usually the type who boasted of a woman's attentions. But he could still picture Cameron walking out of the restaurant with Lydia, his arm around her, looking so cozy and comfortable together.

He'd been startled by the surge of raw possessiveness he felt when he'd seen Lydia with Cameron. He hadn't been prepared for the emotion, hadn't quite known how to deal with it. He'd been trying to figure it out ever since, trying to convince himself that what he felt for Lydia was only friendship. They had a good thing going between them. It would be a shame to ruin it with a lot of messy emotions that couldn't really lead anywhere between two equally driven workaholics.

But it still felt pretty good to let Cameron know that Lydia had been with him during his illness.

"Sounds as if you're in good hands," Cameron murmured.

Lydia appeared in the doorway at that moment, mouthing the words, "Dinner's ready."

"Yes," he said to Cameron. "Very good hands."

"I'll let you go, then. Take care of yourself, pal. Let me know if you need anything."

"Thanks, Cam." Scott replaced the phone in its cradle, his gaze locked with Lydia's. He believed he was feeling a little better—as long as Lydia was there with him.

Chapter Ten

Scott's appetite was still well below normal, but Lydia was satisfied that he made an effort to eat some of the light meal she'd prepared for them. Afterward, they sat for a while in his living room, talking comfortably about anything that occurred to them.

Lydia was fascinated when Scott showed her his rather extensive collection of old Parker fountain pens. She hadn't known about this particular collection and she found it very interesting. He proved to be quite an expert, describing the history of each type of pen, including the year it debuted. The most valuable pen in his collection, he confided, was a 1945 Parker 51 black double-jewel in near mint condition. She didn't know what that meant, but it sounded impressive, and she held the instrument very carefully when he handed it to her to examine.

She was particularly intrigued that so many of the pens were engraved. She could have spent hours studying the tiny messages and thinking about these gifts between people who were probably long dead.

Scott had been sitting upright on the couch, but he began to slide sideways after they put the pens away. Lydia handed him a pillow for his head.

"I can't believe I'm so weak that getting out of bed for a little while totally wipes me out," he complained.

"You can't expect miracles. You've been very sick. It's going to be a few more days before you have all your strength back."

He shook his head against the pillow, a stubborn frown on his face. ''I'm feeling much better. I'll be able to work tomorrow.''

''I don't think so.''

''Sure I will. I just need another night to sleep it off.''

''Surely you can take a sick day or two.''

''Doesn't look good. Potential partners don't give in to illness.''

''And how does it look when potential partners collapse in the middle of a meeting?''

''I won't collapse.''

He couldn't even sit upright for more than an hour, she realized, looking at him sprawled on the couch. There was no way he'd be able to work the next day, but she decided not to waste any more time arguing about it. He would figure it out for himself when he woke up tomorrow morning. ''Just try not to overdo it,'' she said.

Scott pushed himself up again, swinging his feet to the floor. ''As much as I appreciate everything you've done for me this weekend, you should probably go home, Lydia. There's no need for you to stay tonight—I'm feeling better and you need to rest so you can work tomorrow.''

She studied him for a moment, seeing the lingering signs of his illness but knowing he was right. ''You're sure you'll be okay?''

''I'll be fine.''

''I want you to take some more medicine before I go. I'll leave a glass of water beside your bed in case you get thirsty during the night. And I'm putting my number on your speed dial so you can call me quickly if you need me.''

He was watching her with a faint smile and a warm glow in his eyes that seemed to have nothing to do with fever. ''Thank you, Lydia. I hope I haven't interfered too badly with your work.''

''Actually, I've finished everything I wanted to accomplish this weekend,'' she said with a self-conscious little shrug. ''I worked while you slept—and generally without interruption. The only chore I skipped was a trip to the grocery store, and I can do that on the way home from work tomorrow.''

"I hope *you* don't get sick. That really would interfere with your schedule."

"I've been careful to wash my hands frequently," she assured him.

"With antibacterial soap, I hope," he said, his expression serious.

She almost sighed. "Your illness was caused by a virus, not bacteria. Antibacterial agents are useless against viruses. Plain soap and water are the most effective means of—"

Scott laughed hoarsely in genuine amusement. "Sorry, Lydia. I was teasing. I *have* learned a lot from the things you've told me...such as the difference between viruses and bacteria."

She did sigh then. Loudly. "You certainly knew which button to push to set me off, didn't you? I suppose you think you're very clever."

"As a matter of fact..."

She stood, giving him a stern look, but secretly pleased that he felt well enough to tease her again. It made her feel a little better about leaving. "Let's get you ready for bed," she said without stopping to think. She should have known better since he was already in a teasing mood.

Scott rose, planted his feet firmly to counteract his lingering weakness and gave her a creditable leer. "I've been waiting all day for you to make that offer. You *are* going to join me, aren't you?"

Determined to hold her own with him, she raised her eyebrows. "You're in no shape to do anything even if I took you up on that challenge."

His teeth flashed. "Why don't you come with me and find out?"

She searched for a sufficiently witty and sophisticated answer, but then she laughed when Scott swayed and reached out to clutch the couch for support. "Definitely all talk," she said, and moved to help him.

"Okay, maybe you're right, for tonight at least. How about giving me a rain check?"

"You're delirious. Maybe I should call your sister and let her know."

He winced. "Ouch. Low blow, Lydia."

"Mmm. At least I know how to keep you in line."

Some fifteen minutes later, Scott was sitting on the edge of his bed, his pills, a glass of water and his cordless telephone all close at hand.

"Is there anything else you need?" Lydia fretted, still a bit hesitant about leaving him alone.

He smiled crookedly. "There couldn't possibly be anything you've forgotten."

"But if you *do* need me—"

"I'll call." He reached out to take her hand. "Stop worrying, Lydia. You've done so much for me already. I don't know how to thank you."

She smiled rather tremulously, all too conscious of the contact between them. "You've thanked me several times," she reminded him lightly, self-consciously. "I really haven't done that much."

"I won't even dignify that foolish remark with an argument." He tugged at her hand until she leaned toward him, then cupped the back of her head with his free hand. "You're a very special person, Lydia McKinley," he said against her cheek. "I'm very fortunate to have you for a friend."

Her face flushed with a fever of her own. He kissed the soft spot just below her ear, avoiding contact with her mouth—probably to spare her from infection, she thought.

"Good night," he said, his voice an intimate murmur.

She was almost overcome with the urge to wrap her arms around him and lay her head on his broad shoulder. To kiss his sexy mouth and the heck with infection and viruses and potential heartbreak. It took every ounce of willpower she had to make herself straighten and step away from him. "Good night, Scott."

She didn't look back as she turned and left the room. She was afraid she wouldn't be able to leave at all if she did.

Scott was still awake when Heather called a short time after Lydia left. He had been lying on his back, staring at the bedroom ceiling and thinking of Lydia getting ready for bed above him and cursing his body for making him crave something he was in no condition to pursue.

"Are you feeling any better?" Heather asked as soon as he answered.

"Much better," he lied, ignoring his many discomforts.

"You're sure? Because Steve said it can take several days—a week or more, sometimes—to rebound from the flu."

He had no intention of being down that long. "You know me. I'm too stubborn to let a flu bug get the better of me. I'll be back at work tomorrow."

"Don't rush yourself, Scott. Steve said there can be serious complications if you neglect your health now."

"I've had excellent care. I'm not expecting any complications." Not from the flu anyway, he added silently, glancing toward the ceiling again.

"Is Lydia still there?"

"No. I sent her home to get some rest. She

wouldn't have gone if she thought there was any reason to worry.''

''She's been very kind to take such good care of you while you were sick,'' Heather admitted a bit grudgingly.

''Yes, she has. Do you see now how unfair you were to dislike her without even knowing her?''

''I never said I didn't like her. I merely said I thought she was wrong for you. I still think so, even if she has been so nice to take care of you.''

Scott's head was starting to hurt again, and it had more to do with his sister than his illness. ''Lydia and I are only good friends, but I still can't imagine why you aren't trying to push me into her arms. You said you thought she'd be great for Cameron. What's the big difference?''

''Cameron's more like Lydia. He's more reserved, his emotions more guarded than yours. It wouldn't bother him that she's the same way. You would need more reassurance. If you took the risk of trusting a woman with your heart, you'd need to know she feels the same way. That's why you've been so careful since Tammy hurt you in law school. It's why you weren't particularly upset when your affair with That Woman ended—you both made it clear that it wasn't going anywhere. I'm not sure you would ever know Lydia's true emotions. I don't think you could ever feel certain that her feelings wouldn't change with circumstances.''

Scott had listened to Heather's rambling in reluctant fascination, but he jumped in when she finally paused for breath. ''You've been watching daytime TV again, haven't you?''

Heather sighed. ''You aren't taking me seriously.''

''Do you actually expect me to? You're an account executive, not a shrink. And you don't know Lydia well enough to analyze her, even if you knew what the hell you were talking about. Nor do you know what I need or want from a relationship. Concentrate on your own love life, Heather. I'll take care of mine.''

''All I'm saying is—''

"I really don't feel like getting into this again tonight. I'm going to take a pill and go to sleep so I'll feel more like myself tomorrow."

The reminder of his illness made her drop the subject. "You're right. I shouldn't be arguing with you while you're still feeling so bad. For the record, I am grateful to Lydia for all she's done this weekend since you were too pigheaded to call and let me take care of you."

"Good night, Heather."

Resigned, she replied, "Good night, Scott. I'll check with you tomorrow."

He was shaking his head when he hung up the phone. Heather could be so full of it sometimes, he thought with affectionate exasperation. He didn't know why he even bothered to listen to her when she got off on such absurd tangents.

Scott didn't make it to work Monday. Nor was he up to the effort Tuesday. By Wednesday, though, he was well enough to spend most of the day at his office, where he pretended to be completely recovered and worked until he was close to dropping trying to catch up.

He didn't know how he'd have gotten through those days without Lydia. She was there every day, checking on him before she left for work, making sure he had medicine, food and drinks on hand. Heather called frequently, as well, but didn't feel compelled to hover over him because Lydia was close at hand—another favor he owed Lydia, he thought.

Lydia rang his doorbell Wednesday a half hour after he got home. When he opened the door, she took one look at him and shook her head. "I told you it was too soon for you to go back to work."

"Do I look that bad?"

She studied him closely. "Just really tired. Is there anything you need before I leave you to rest? Do you have anything for dinner?"

"Actually, no. I was thinking about ordering a pizza. Would you like to join me?"

"Well, I—"

"You have to eat," he urged. "This way,

there's no need for you to cook or clean up afterward.''

``All right. I'll just go put these things in my apartment.'' She had apparently stopped by on her way in from the parking lot, her arms still loaded with the work she always brought home with her. ``And I have a couple of quick calls to make,'' she added.

``Let's say an hour, then. I'll place the order. By the time you put your things away, make your calls and change into more comfortable clothes, it should be here. Any special requests for toppings?''

``No hot peppers, please.''

``Sissy mouth, huh?''

``Definitely.''

He watched her turn and walk away, then closed the door. As weary as he had been a few minutes earlier, he was reenergized by the thought of spending time with Lydia that evening.

She had taken care of him long enough, he decided. It was time he did something for Lydia. He picked up the phone.

* * *

Dressed in a long-sleeved T-shirt and jeans, Lydia rang Scott's doorbell again an hour later. She hadn't meant to spend another evening with him; she had only intended to check on him when she stopped by earlier. But he'd looked so tired, and the thought of sharing a pizza with her had seemed to perk him up a bit for some reason. Maybe he just didn't want to eat alone when he still wasn't feeling very well. In which case, there had really been no reason to turn him down.

He opened the door. Surprisingly enough, he looked more rested than he had earlier. Dressed in a loose white shirt and khaki cargo pants, his dark auburn hair attractively tousled around his face, he looked much more like the fit, virile man she had known before the flu had temporarily sidelined him. Something about the gleam in his eyes when he drew her inside his apartment made her realize that Scott was back in the game.

She swallowed and wondered if it was too late to make an excuse and escape to the safety of her own apartment.

Still holding her hand, he led her into the kitchen, where a nice surprise awaited her. He'd set the pizza and a tossed salad on the table, along with his nicest dishes and delicate wineglasses. He'd even lit candles, adding a touch of elegance to the simple meal.

"All this for me?" she asked lightly, trying to conceal how much the gesture meant to her.

"One more thing." He reached into the pantry and brought out a dozen yellow roses in a green glass vase. "These are for you."

He had done it again. She never should have let him know she had a weakness for roses, she thought with a lump in her throat. She simply couldn't resist leaning over to draw in a deep breath of the rich scent. "You shouldn't keep doing this," she murmured. "But thank you."

"After all you did for me, a few flowers are the least I can give you in return." He took the roses and set them on the table between the candles. "We should eat before the food gets cold," he said, holding her chair for her.

She sank into the chair, determined not to

let this get to her. He was just being especially nice because she'd helped him out while he was ill. A pizza dinner was hardly a reason for her to melt at his feet.

After making sure she was seated comfortably, he moved to the counter and pushed a button on a small CD player he'd placed there. Soft, bluesy music poured from the speakers, providing ambience without being intrusive on conversation.

Okay, she thought. He'd added romantic music to the equation. She could handle this—maybe.

She helped herself to the food as he took his seat. The sooner they finished dinner, the sooner she could run like the coward she was. Though he still showed some evidence of his illness, he was no longer weakened by fever, meekly depending on her to take care of him.

Scott was well enough now for her to be wary of him again.

"Wine?" he said, picking up the bottle. "It's a nice red, one of my favorites with pizza."

She rarely drank wine, but after he'd gone to so much trouble… "Just a small glass."

The wine was good, and so was the food. But then, anything probably would have tasted good considering the circumstances, she decided. Candlelight, wine, roses, music, a charming companion… A woman of lesser willpower might have found herself being seduced.

"This isn't exactly what I was expecting when you said we were going to kick off our shoes and eat pizza," she said.

He grinned. "As much as I've enjoyed your attentions for the past few days, I thought it was time to give you a break. I'd have liked to prepare a fancier meal for you, but my cooking skills are rather limited, and the few recipes I've learned to put together take a while."

"This is perfect," she assured him. "I like pizza and I don't have it very often. But you really didn't have to go to so much trouble."

"I set the table and lit the candles," he answered wryly. "That's pretty much the extent of it."

He'd done much more than that, she thought, keeping her gaze on her plate. He had touched her.

Trying to keep everything normal between them, she asked, "How did you manage at work today? Was it difficult?"

He shrugged. "I have a lot of hours to put in to catch up, but I got a pretty good start today."

"You didn't get too tired?"

"No." Something in his tone let her know he was tired of being treated as an invalid. "How was *your* day?" he asked, turning the tables.

"Not as hectic as usual."

"Good. And how's your thesis coming along?"

"I'll keep polishing it until the last possible minute, but everything's pretty much on schedule."

He lifted his wineglass and smiled at her. "To Dr. McKinley."

Dr. McKinley, she thought, taking a sip of her wine. She'd been pursuing the title for a long time. Maybe that was why she felt a little hollow at the thought of actually attaining the degree. Why her most compelling reaction was the question—then what?

Scott asked another question about her work and then another. Almost before Lydia realized it, they were involved in a lively discussion that made her think of the first few times they'd met for dinner and conversation. She'd always found Scott easy to talk to—at least, she had before they complicated everything by dating. Even if the dates had been intended as protection from their matchmaking sisters.

She had other male friends, but she and Scott always connected unusually well. He seemed to understand her. He laughed at her rare jokes and shared many of her interests. She found herself relaxing during the meal, enjoying it immensely. She even accepted a second glass of wine after Scott reminded her humorously that she didn't have to drive home.

When she'd eaten all she could, she pushed her plate away. "I'm full," she said, shaking her head when he offered more.

"I have ice cream for dessert," he said, shamelessly exploiting another of her weaknesses. "Fudge ripple."

She groaned. "I can't eat another bite."

"Maybe you'll want some later."

She glanced at her watch. "I really should be going. I've been neglecting my laundry and housekeeping the past few days."

"And that's my fault, I'm afraid. You've been taking care of me. Would you like me to come up and wash a load of towels to repay you?"

She laughed. "No, thank you. This dinner was payment enough. It was the most relaxing evening I've spent in a while."

She automatically started to clear the kitchen, but Scott refused to allow her to do anything. Telling her he would take care of it later, he carried her roses into the living room, where he set them on the coffee table. "I don't want you to forget these when you go," he said, turning to her with a smile.

"They really are beautiful. I'd be surprised

if there are any roses left in Dallas after all you've given me.''

He chuckled. ''It's hardly been that many.''

She really should go. There was no reason to stay any longer. She had things to do and she was sure Scott did, too. He probably needed to rest—although she couldn't help noticing that he looked perfectly fine. It was hard to tell now that he'd ever been ill.

She was glad he was feeling better—she really was, she assured herself. But she would miss the time they had spent together during the past week, now that there was no good reason for them to continue.

She smoothed her hands down her jeans. ''Well…thank you again for dinner.''

He stepped closer, lifting a hand to brush her cheek with his fingertips. ''It was my pleasure.''

She swallowed. It amazed her how that simple brush of his hand affected her. She'd touched him dozens of times during the past few days. She'd tested the warmth of his skin for fever, steadied him when he walked, helped him take medicine and drink juice. While she'd been aware of him during that time, she'd been more concerned with his comfort than her reactions to him.

Yet this simple touch made her head spin.

She couldn't think of anything to say. Funny how often that happened when he stood so close to her. She just stood there, looking up at him, wondering what he was thinking as he gazed back at her, his fingers still lying against her cheek.

Scott's smile faded. His eyes darkened. His other hand rose, his fingers spreading to cup her face between his palms.

She should have moved away. Should have reminded him that this wasn't the sort of relationship they had. That they had agreed not to complicate things this way.

As his mouth lowered very slowly to hers she realized that things were about to become *very* complicated.

With only a little pressure, he lifted her mouth to his. She went up on tiptoe, resting her hands on his chest to steady herself. His lips brushed hers, hardly touching her. He taunted her with the embrace, giving just enough to make her want more. She parted her lips in silent invitation, but he continued to hold back, the kiss only a promise of what it could be.

She might have pulled back if he'd come on too strong, if he'd expected too much. Instead, she stayed, tantalized by possibilities. Her fingers curled into his shirt in involuntary demand.

Still holding her face between his hands, he tilted her face higher and nibbled at her mouth. Teasing, enticing nibbles that made her tremble, made her lips soften and quiver beneath his. A faint sound escaped her—it should have been a protest but sounded more like a plea. Only then did Scott wrap his arms around her, pull her tightly against him and kiss her exactly the way she wanted—needed—him to kiss her.

Her arms locked around his neck. Precariously poised on her toes, she leaned into him, feeling the contact from her breasts to her thighs. *Strong,* she thought. *Solid.*

And aroused.

He wanted her. And she could no longer deny that she wanted him, too.

His tongue slipped between her lips, deepening the kiss until she could think of nothing but what was happening right then. How could she worry about perils or consequences when this felt so very good, so very right? The kiss was so perfect, so special—and she was so tempted to let it go on, to experience the full range of feelings and emotions she knew Scott could introduce her to. Things she had only dreamed of before.

But Lydia wasn't the if-it-feels-good-do-it type. Never had been. And she couldn't change who she was during the course of one spectacular kiss.

Trembling with reluctance, she pulled her mouth from beneath his and pushed lightly against him, needing space. He hesitated only an instant before loosening his arms, the pause just long enough to let her know he'd briefly considered resisting.

He kept his hands on her shoulders as he gazed down at her. "I've been wanting to do that for a long time now," he murmured.

She swallowed and moistened her still-unsteady lips. "I—"

"I want you, Lydia."

The carefully worded speech she'd intended dissolved in her mind. Knowing he felt that way had been disconcerting enough; hearing him actually say the words staggered her. "Scott—"

"You need time," he said.

She nodded. She needed time. She needed distance. She needed perspective. God help her, she needed *him.* And while that was her most immediate requirement, she knew the others must come first.

She nodded. "I have to think about this," she whispered. "Before it goes any further—I have to think."

"I know. You aren't comfortable acting on impulse. You have to decide first if the benefits are worth the risks. I can wait until you come up with the answer," he said, gently touching her cheek again, "but I hope you'll decide to give it a try."

It shook her even more that he seemed to understand her so well. And that he seemed to be making no effort to change what he knew about her. She was more accustomed to impatience and frustration from men who had wanted her before. Which made Scott all the more difficult to resist.

It took more willpower than she'd ever needed before to step away from him. "I'd better go."

He nodded, obviously reluctant, but resigned. "All right. I hope to hear from you soon. And, Lydia...?"

She had already taken a step toward the door. "Yes?"

"This has nothing to do with our sisters. It's strictly between us."

She studied his face, seeing the desire he wasn't trying to hide from her. "I know," she whispered, forcing herself to take another step toward the door.

"Don't forget your roses."

Without looking at him again—probably because she was afraid she wouldn't be able to leave at all if she did—she took the vase from him, then all but bolted out the door when he opened it.

"We'll talk later," he called after her.

She only hoped she would know what to say when they did.

Chapter Eleven

Lydia happened to be in her office when Gary Dunston called Thursday afternoon. ''How have you been?'' he asked.

''Fine, thank you. And you?'' she inquired politely, dreading what she knew was coming. When she hadn't heard from him after the reception at his bookstore, she decided he'd reached the same conclusion she had—that they had almost nothing in common. She never really expected to hear from him again—and wasn't at all bothered by the probability.

''To be honest,'' he said in the overly diffident tone she associated with him, ''I've been trying to come up with the nerve to call you again. I know you didn't have a very good time at my reception—''

''I told you it was a very interesting evening,'' she said, guiltily compelled to reassure him.

''Yes, I know you did. That's because you're such a kind and gracious person.''

She winced, feeling even worse because she found his compliments more annoying than endearing.

''And because you *are* so nice,'' he continued doggedly, ''I was hoping you would give me another chance to show you a good time. Larissa said you enjoy the theater. There's a community theater production of *Guys and Dolls* tomorrow night. Would you like to go with me?''

She loved the theater. She liked *Guys and Dolls.* The problem was, she didn't think she could spend another evening with Gary. She debated between being totally honest with him or making a polite excuse. Her policy was usually honesty—but Gary seemed so shy and sensitive that she almost felt as if she'd be kicking a puppy if she wasn't very careful with his feelings. "I'm sorry, Gary, but I'm afraid I can't. I already have plans for this weekend."

His silence told her that she had hurt him even though she'd tried not to. "I see," he said after a time. "You're, um, seeing someone else?"

She wouldn't tell him, of course, that she'd spent most of the preceding night trying to decide whether she wanted to begin an affair with Scott Pearson. A calculated, no-strings, no-future affair based on an attraction stronger than anything she'd felt for any man before him. She couldn't tell Gary that she'd almost convinced herself it would be worth the inevitable pain just to experience a blazing, passionate, unpredictable affair for once in her otherwise careful and goal-oriented life. No matter how fleeting the relationship turned out to be.

"I simply have other plans," she said, deciding that was all the explanation she needed to give. ''But thank you for asking, Gary.''

''Of course. Another time, perhaps?''

Honesty had to be the kindest option, she decided. ''I don't think so,'' she said as gently as possible.

His heavy sigh carried clearly through the phone line. ''I see.''

''I'm sorry.''

''I understand. It isn't easy for a guy like me to compete with the man who was with you at your sister's party. She told me you aren't involved with him—but she was wrong, wasn't she?''

Lydia didn't answer. It was, after all, none of his business whether she was involved with Scott or not—especially since she didn't even know the answer at this point.

''I guess Larissa was indulging in wishful thinking. She thinks the lawyer is all wrong for you. She's afraid he'll hurt you. She said he's a user and a shallow charmer—and that you aren't used to dealing with men like that.''

Gary was beginning to sound sullen and resentful. As if there had been a serious competition between the two men and Gary had come out the loser. She refused to be drawn into a discussion with him about Scott. "If you'll excuse me, Gary, I have a class. I don't want to be late. Goodbye."

She hung up without giving him a chance to respond. She really did have a class and she had to hurry—but she would be talking to Larissa at the very first opportunity, she promised herself.

Because she decided she couldn't adequately express her indignation over the telephone, Lydia drove straight to her sister's apartment when she left the university. Charlie answered the door. He looked as if he was on his way out; he carried his oboe case in his left hand.

"Lydia. This is a nice surprise." He leaned over to kiss her cheek. "Is this a visit or is there something I can do for you?"

"I need to talk to Larissa. Is she here?"

"She's in her studio. Is something wrong?"

"I just have a bone to pick with my sister. A personal matter."

He smiled crookedly. "Oops. Looks like it's a good thing I have a rehearsal to get to. I make it a practice never to get involved in a sibling squabble."

As annoyed as she was, Lydia couldn't help but smile. "I don't think there'll be any actual bloodshed. Just a few heated words—followed, I hope, by an abject apology from Larissa and a promise never to do it again."

He chuckled sympathetically. "Good luck."

"Thank you."

"I'd better be going. It was good to see you, Lydia. Come back when we have more time to visit."

Because she was quite fond of him, Lydia smiled and agreed. "I'll do that."

Sketching her a funny salute, he let himself out, closing the door behind him.

Lydia found her sister sitting in her studio, staring intently at a half-finished painting. She didn't seem in the least surprised to see Lydia.

"What do you think of it?" she demanded, motioning toward the canvas.

"Needs more red. Larissa, I—"

"More red?" Larissa frowned and twisted a strand of hair around her finger. "Why?"

"You seem to be going for anger. Red makes me think of anger."

"Anger? Not passion?"

"They're very closely connected, aren't they?"

"Maybe a little more purple..."

"More purple's going to cool it off. It needs heat. Red."

"You could be right. You so often are."

Lydia shook her head impatiently. "I didn't stop by to discuss your work."

"Okay. Want some tea?"

"Larissa, I need to talk to you."

"We can talk over tea, can't we?" With one last, thoughtful glance at the canvas, Larissa stood and moved toward the doorway, her loose, brightly colored dress fluttering around her.

Sighing, Lydia followed her sister into the

kitchen. The only way to get through to Larissa was just to start talking. "Gary Dunston called me this afternoon."

Running water into a teakettle, Larissa looked over her shoulder with a bright smile. "That's lovely."

"No, it *isn't* lovely. I do not want to date Gary."

"But, Lyddie, he's such a sweet man. Such a gentle spirit. Why won't you give him a chance?"

"I gave him a chance. I'm not interested, Larissa."

Larissa set the kettle on the stove, heaving a big sigh as she did so. "It's your decision, of course. Whatever I think, it's up to you to decide whether you want to go out with Gary."

"Exactly. And I don't want to—as I told him when he called."

"I hope you were kind."

"I tried to be."

"Sounds as if you've taken care of it, then.

So why are you annoyed with me? *I* didn't tell him to call you today."

"You've been encouraging him."

"Nonsense. I gave him your number after the party and suggested he give you a call sometime. That's the full extent of my involvement."

"You talked to him about Scott."

"He asked if you and Scott were dating exclusively, and I told him what you told me—that you and Scott were only friends."

Lydia shook her head. "That isn't all you told him. He said you confided in him that you weren't happy that Scott and I were dating. It was obvious he knew you don't trust Scott."

A slight frown drew Larissa's brows together. "I didn't tell him all that. I merely said that you and Scott weren't a couple. I suppose he could have read my feelings in my expression—Gary's a very intuitive man." She made it sound like another point in Gary's favor.

"You're sure you didn't say anything negative about Scott to Gary?"

"Of course not, Lyddie. That would have

been rude. Scott was a guest in my home. I suppose Gary assumed I disapproved because I encouraged *him* to call you. Anything else was just speculation on his part...or perhaps his own conclusions after seeing you and Scott together.''

''Whatever his motivation, I didn't like it. I hope I've made that clear to him—and to you.''

Larissa held up her hands in a classic sign of surrender. ''I give up. I promise—no more interfering in your social life. From now on, you're on your own.''

It wasn't exactly an abject apology. But to Lydia's relief at least it sounded as though Larissa was giving up on her matchmaking scheme. That was one less problem for her to deal with now, she thought as she sank into a chair at Larissa's table.

Larissa set a cup of tea in front of her. ''Are you still mad at me?''

Lydia smiled faintly. ''No.''

''Good. So tell me what you've been up to since we talked last.''

Stalling, Lydia took a cautious sip of the very hot tea.

Larissa studied her from across the table, perceptive as always where her sister was concerned. "You've been spending time with him, haven't you? The lawyer."

"His name is Scott. And yes, I've seen a lot of him lately. He's had the flu, and I gave him a hand for a few days."

"So *that's* what's been keeping you too busy to answer your phone lately. I thought you were busy with work."

"With both, actually. I was able to get quite a lot done while I sat with Scott."

"While you sat with him? He must have been quite sick."

"Yes, he was."

"Is he better now?"

Thinking of the strength in Scott's arms when he held her yesterday, Lydia nodded. "He seems to be fully recovered."

"Well, I'm glad to hear that," Larissa said, and Lydia believed her.

Larissa might not approve of lawyers as a

whole, and Scott in particular because he was interested in Lydia, but she wouldn't wish anything unpleasant on him. As blunt and obstinate as she could be, Larissa had a very kind heart.

Larissa set her teacup down, tracing the steamy rim with one paint-stained fingertip. "You're really very fond of him, aren't you, Lyddie? You wouldn't have made so much time to take care of him if you weren't."

"I was simply being a good friend and a good neighbor. He needed help and I—"

"Lydia..."

Larissa's tone and expression told Lydia she was wasting time trying to sidestep the question. "I like him," she answered simply. "Very much."

"Are you sleeping with him?"

Lydia was accustomed enough to her sister's ways not to be overly startled by the blunt question, but it still made her blink. "No."

"Your choice or his?"

"Mine."

"Does that mean he wants you to?"

"Is *nothing* private to you?" Lydia asked in exasperation.

"Not between us. Come on, Lyddie, I talked to you a lot when I first started dating Charlie. You knew how nervous I was about moving in with him, how worried I was that living with someone would interfere with my work. You knew how hard it was for me to trust him to give me the freedom I need even with our lives so intimately connected. I just want to know if you have those same concerns about Scott."

"Not exactly the same," Lydia finally replied. "Scott's too busy with his own career to interfere with mine."

"That's a good thing, isn't it?"

"Of course."

"So...as much as I hate to ask this...what's holding you back? You like him, he obviously likes you, you don't get in each other's way. He isn't involved with anyone else, is he, now that his affair with Cheyenne's friend, Paula, is over?"

"No. There isn't anyone else." She'd spent

enough time with him now to be assured of that.

"You aren't attracted to him?"

Lydia gave her sister a look. "You saw him, Larissa. What do *you* think?"

"I think he isn't my type, but most women would probably appreciate him. What do *you* think?"

"I am definitely attracted to him."

"So...?"

"I'm considering it," Lydia admitted.

"Is that right?" Larissa sipped her tea, studying Lydia over the rim of her cup. "You're thinking of having an affair with him?"

"Let's just say I'm open to the possibility."

"Are you thinking long-term here?"

"I'm hardly in a position for that. You know how unsettled my career is right now. I don't have my doctorate yet and I don't even know where I'll be living in the fall. I have résumés out from Berkeley to Boston and I'm getting replies from several places in between. I'm not even renewing my lease when it runs out July 1. This is no time for me to enter *anything* long-term.''

''A fling, then.''

Lydia didn't really like that term, either, but she supposed it described what she was considering as well as any. ''I don't know, Larissa. I'm so busy and my time is split so many ways already. It's probably best if Scott and I just remain friends.''

If that was possible, she added silently, remembering the kisses that had spontaneously erupted between them the day before.

''Then you'll just have to decide whether it's worth making the time, won't you? And worth the risk of getting involved even temporarily with this lawyer.''

''Larissa...''

''Okay, I know his name. Scott. You'll have to decide whether Scott is worth the risk. And you'll have to decide on your own—I've promised to stay out of it.''

Lydia smiled across the table at her beautiful, brilliant and bossy sister. ''Just don't stay too far away, sis.''

Larissa returned the smile with a very sweet one of her own. ‘‘You couldn’t keep me very far away. Even if you got yourself a lawyer.’’

Lydia couldn’t help but laugh.

Scott all but dragged himself into his apartment Thursday evening, so tired from a long day in court and at his office that he could hardly put one foot in front of the other. He hated this lingering weakness left over from his illness. He’d managed to conceal it in front of his colleagues, but now that he was alone, he collapsed onto his bed and groaned. For a young man in supposedly excellent physical condition, he certainly was wiped out.

He found himself wearily rephrasing an old Eric Clapton song—he’d fought the flu and the flu won.

Finally recovering enough to move, he rolled to his side and punched the play button on his answering machine, which indicated that there was one message. The sound of Lydia’s voice reenergized him.

He swung his legs over the side of the bed to raise the volume.

''Scott? Hi, it's Lydia. I, um, just wanted to see how you're feeling. And to see if maybe we can take in that movie you've mentioned this weekend. So anyway, give me a call when you have time. Bye.''

The machine clicked to silence. Scott was smiling by the time the message ended, his exhaustion forgotten. He reached for the phone.

Scott couldn't quite figure out what Lydia was thinking on the following Saturday evening—the first time both of them had been free to get together. They had seen a movie—a fairly decent romantic comedy—and decided afterward to stop for ice cream. A casual evening, very low-key. No reason at all for Lydia to be nervous—and yet she seemed to be all evening. Why? Because this was their first ''real'' date? Because of the kisses they'd shared a few days earlier? Or because of the ones he hoped would come later?

As he drove away from the ice-cream parlor,

he glanced at her out of the corner of his eye. She was sitting very straight, very still, in the passenger seat of his car, her hands linked tightly in her lap. Keeping his left hand on the wheel, he reached out to cover both of hers with his right. Her hands felt so cold. He curled his hand around hers, trying to warm her.

"What's wrong, Lydia?"

"Nothing," she assured him a bit too quickly.

"You're sure?"

"Yes, of course. It's been a very nice evening."

"So you aren't feeling the least uncomfortable right now?"

"No, not at all."

He laughed and lifted her left hand to his lips. "Liar," he murmured against her knuckles.

She didn't dignify the accusation with an answer—but he noticed that a small smile softened the corner of her mouth. He laced his fingers with hers and lowered their linked hands to the console between them. He was pleased that she didn't seem to want to break that contact, her fingers curling lightly around his.

He didn't let her go until he turned into the parking lot of their apartment complex. He noted that she clenched her hands in her lap again as he pulled into his parking space. She looked suddenly nervous again. Oddly enough, he felt his own nerves suddenly thrumming.

"How about some coffee?" he asked, trying to keep his tone light, undemanding. "I can make some for us in only a few minutes."

He found himself holding his breath during the several long moments she hesitated. There was a lot more at stake than a cup of coffee—and they both knew it. Just as they knew the movie wasn't the only reason they had gotten together that evening. The question was, had she reconsidered since she called him? He only hoped he could be gracious about it if she had, even though he would be extremely disappointed.

Lydia finally broke the silence. "Make that decaf and you're on."

He was pleased to note that her voice was firm and steady, no nervousness evident now. He wanted her to be very sure of the step they were taking. He wanted no regrets to spoil their special friendship.

He opened his car door, and Lydia followed suit. They met again at the front of the car, and Scott took her hand again as he led her toward his apartment.

Having been a nervous wreck all evening, Lydia was surprisingly calm when she stepped into Scott's living room. She had made her choice, she thought with a deep, steadying breath. She wouldn't change her mind.

She spoke with a faint smile. "Scott?"

He was already moving toward the kitchen. He paused and glanced over his shoulder. "Yes?"

"I don't really want any coffee."

Very slowly, he turned to face her, an expression in his eyes that made her heart suddenly start to beat faster. "What *do* you want, Lydia?"

He was certainly putting her newfound confidence to the test. She lifted her chin, steadily meeting his gaze. "You."

His smile started slowly, deepening the corners of his mouth, then curving into a full, enticingly dimpled grin. "A good host tries to provide everything his guest desires."

It was just like him to make a joke when it was taking all her courage to keep from running and hiding behind a chair or something. She wrinkled her nose at him. "Just be quiet and come here."

He laughed. "Yes, ma'am."

A moment later, she was in his arms, and his mouth was on hers. The cocky humor was gone now. He kissed her with the urgency that had been simmering just beneath the surface between them all evening.

Lydia locked her arms around his neck, parting her lips to deepen the kiss. She buried her hands in his hair, loving the softness and thickness of it. And then she lowered them, sliding her palms across his broad shoulders and down his back to his narrow waist. Every inch of him felt good to her. Perfect, actually. She'd never seen a more beautiful, more perfect man.

And for tonight, she thought, pulling him closer, he was hers.

He broke off the kiss and rested his forehead against hers. "Lydia," he murmured, "you make my head spin."

She smiled. "Are you sure that's not a lingering result of your flu?"

"I do seem to have a fever again," he acknowledged ruefully. "But this time it's caused by you, not the flu."

He touched his lips to her forehead, then dragged them slowly to her temple and down the side of her face to the corner of her mouth. He left a trail of heat in his wake, making her face feel flushed and hot. "I think I have a fever, too," she whispered against his lips.

"You took care of me. Now it's my turn to take care of you."

She gasped in surprise when he swung her suddenly into his arms. Any worry she'd had about whether he'd fully recovered his strength was now assuaged. His arms were as solid as steel around her, supporting her so easily that she had no fear he would drop her as he moved toward his bedroom.

"I'm perfectly capable of making this walk by your side," she felt compelled to tell him.

He paused to smile at her. "I know you are. Would you like to do so?"

Her own smile felt tremulous. "No. I just wanted to make it clear."

Moments later, he set her on her feet beside the bed. "I have wanted this since you spilled your papers at my feet and I helped you pick them up," he told her. "When we had those early dinners and talked about DNA, I sat there and marveled at how beautiful and brilliant you are. And I wanted you then."

She wasn't beautiful. But she didn't intend to argue with him about it now since she liked hearing him say it. "Are you telling me you had an ulterior motive when you suggested our 'standby escort' plan?"

He brushed a strand of hair away from her

face, leaving his fingertips at her temple. ‘‘Maybe not consciously. But I knew even then that I wanted to spend more time with you.’’

She figured his honesty should be reciprocated. ‘‘I kept telling myself—and everyone else—that I only wanted to be your friend. That there was not, and never would be, anything more between us. I almost convinced myself that was all I wanted it to be. It turned out I was lying—to everyone else, and to myself.’’

He leaned over to kiss her, lingering until her lips warmed and softened beneath his. ‘‘I’m glad you’re my friend, Lydia McKinley. And I’m very glad we’ve decided to be more than friends.’’

She only hoped they would still be friends when the affair ended.

Putting the fleeting fear out of her mind, she decided they had talked long enough. She reached out to release the top button of his shirt and then the next. She hadn’t been able to get the sight of his bare chest out of her mind; now she wanted to feel him beneath her hands.

He stood very still and let her finish the task without interference. She took her time, savoring the pleasure of revealing him in magnificent inches. Pulling the shirt from the waistband of his slacks, she spread her hands beneath it, the light dusting of hair on his chest tickling her palms and making her smile. He felt so good that she thought he would probably taste even better. She leaned forward to find out.

She felt the lazy amusement leave him with the first light nip of her teeth. By the time she had nibbled her way from his throat to his right nipple, he had visibly tensed. She ran her tongue across the firm, flat disk, secretly delighted when he quivered in reaction. She slid the shirt off his shoulders, letting it fall to the floor at their feet. And then she reached for his belt buckle.

Scott's patience had obviously run out. Lydia found herself suddenly flat on her back on the bed, her sweater being pulled over her head, Scott's mouth at her breasts. She didn't want to think about the practice it must have taken for him to strip them both so swiftly and skillfully out of their clothes. For him to know exactly where and how to touch her to melt her bones and turn her brain to pudding. However he had attained his expertise, she could only be grateful now that he was sharing it so generously with her.

He explored her with his hands, his mouth, his body, until she demanded more. Efficiently donning protection, he gave her everything she asked for—and so much more.

Sensations cascaded through her like fireworks in a summer sky, glittering so brightly they were almost painful in their beauty and intensity. Exploding into brilliant bursts of feelings and emotions that made her cry out in helpless wonder.

And then she gathered her strength and created a few fireworks of her own. There was a deep sense of satisfaction when she pulled a hoarse groan from deep within Scott's chest.

All in all, she thought, collapsing bonelessly

against his still-heaving chest, it had been a
spectacular show. And, as she had predicted
it was like nothing she had ever experience
before.

Already she wondered when she would experience it again.

Scott's hand moved idly in her hair, stroking, caressing, soothing them both with the
gentle motion. "You never cease to amaze me
Lydia McKinley," he murmured.

She smiled against his shoulder. "I coul
say the same about you."

He stroked his thumb along the line of he
jaw, from her ear to her chin. "Will you stay
with me tonight?"

Frowning, she thought about it. "I'm no
sure that's a habit we want to get into."

"I only asked for tonight," he reminded her
a faint touch of amusement in his voice.

Had she taken too much for granted with her
cautious response? A little embarrassed, she
mimicked his light tone. "Yes, well, give a
guy like you an inch..."

He chuckled and kissed the top of her head

"You may be right. But will you stay for at least tonight?"

It probably wasn't a bright idea. Definitely not a good precedent to set. But it felt so right to lie beside him, their limbs tangled, their hearts still beating in rhythm. Maybe—just for tonight—she would stay.

She settled her cheek more comfortably into his shoulder. "I'm not sure I have the energy to climb the stairs anyway."

"I'll take that as a yes." He rolled to lean over her. "And since you're here..."

He moved a hand to her breasts, and Lydia arched involuntarily into his touch. Perhaps she had some energy left after all.

Chapter Twelve

The morning sun slipped slowly into Scott's bedroom, creeping across the floor until the shadows of the night retreated to the far corners. Scott had been awake for a while propped on one elbow while he watched Lydia sleep.

He doubted that she would appreciate his observing her while she was so unguarded, so vulnerable. But he couldn't help it. Looking at her gave him so much pleasure.

She slept on her stomach, her arms beneath her pillow. Her face was turned toward him her cheek softly flushed, her lips slightly parted. Her silky brown hair was tousled appealingly around her face, one strand lying enticingly close to the corner of her mouth. He was tempted to brush it back, but he didn't want to risk waking her. Not yet.

It was too nice just to lie there, savoring the sight of Lydia McKinley in his bed.

He didn't want to ruin the moment with too much analysis. But he knew that his feelings for Lydia were unexpectedly complex, different from what he'd felt for the women he'd been involved with before. It wasn't the somewhat detached, rather cynical affection he'd felt for Paula, nor the starry-eyed, almost painful infatuation with Tammy. This was unique. Just as Lydia was.

He didn't know exactly how to label it or how long it would last. He only knew that one night with her wouldn't be enough.

Lydia's eyelashes fluttered, then slowly lifted. He watched as consciousness returned to her in increments until she was fully aware of where she was and who was lying beside her. And then he smiled. ‘‘Good morning.’’

‘‘Good morning.’’ Her voice was husky from sleep.

He liked hearing it that way. ‘‘Did you sleep well?’’

‘‘Surprisingly enough, yes.’’

‘‘Why are you surprised?’’

‘‘I don’t usually sleep well in a strange bed,’’ she admitted.

He tried to keep the smugness out of his voice. ‘‘I suppose you were exhausted.’’

Her tone was dry when she answered. ‘‘I suppose I was.’’

He finally reached out to brush back the lock of hair that had been tempting him. Once his fingers touched her, he didn’t want to pull his hand away. ‘‘Do you have plans for today? Will you spend the afternoon with me?’’

‘‘I’d like that,’’ she said, catching his hand in hers. And then she frowned. ‘‘No, I’m sorry. I can’t.’’

‘‘Why not?’’

"I have a study group meeting this afternoon."

"Tonight, then. We could have dinner, maybe—"

"No. Tonight I'm speaking at a meeting for microbiologists. It's the end of a weekend retreat. I was actually supposed to be there yesterday, but I begged off."

Because of him, he thought. He shouldn't complain that she had no time today when she'd already given so much. Lydia was a very busy woman—he'd known that all along. And that was exactly what he'd wanted, right? Someone too busy with her own life to interfere with his.

"What time does your study group meet?"

"Two o'clock."

He shifted to lean over her. "That gives us some time, then."

Sliding her arms around his neck, she looked up at him with mock innocence. "Time for what?"

His mouth hovering an inch over hers, he smiled. "For whatever turns us on."

She laughed and reached up to take his head between her hands. ''You turn me on, Scott Pearson,'' she murmured as she pulled his mouth to hers.

He was very glad to hear that. He would hate to be in this condition alone.

More than a week later, during the first week of May, Lydia found herself wondering if a woman could be technically having an affair if she never actually saw the man with whom she was supposedly involved.

She had hardly spoken with Scott since the night they'd spent together. Extremely busy with the demands of their respective careers, they hardly had a chance to breathe during those days, much less spend time with each other. It seemed that every time Lydia had an evening free, Scott was busy, and vice versa. Even the weekends, during which they had found time to be together before, were suddenly filled with obligations. It was as if forces were at work to deliberately keep them apart, Lydia thought wearily.

She wondered if she should take that as a sign.

"We weren't kidding ourselves when we said we didn't have time for anyone in our lives, were we?" Scott asked over the phone after another evening ruined by a last-minute crisis at his office.

Sitting in her apartment surrounded by things she needed to do, Lydia swallowed a sigh. "No. Obviously we weren't."

"I want to see you, Lydia."

"You will," she assured him. "As soon as we're both free."

"How does Thursday evening look for you?"

"I'm leaving town early Thursday morning. I won't be back until Saturday afternoon."

"Where to this time?" he asked in resignation.

"Michigan. I'm interviewing at the university Friday."

"Michigan?" His tone suddenly sounded strained. "That's, um, a long way."

"Yes."

"Quite a change of climate for a Texas gal. Think you can handle those winters?"

"I'm sure I could. But there's no guarantee I'll get the job. I'm not even sure I'm one of the front-runners for this one."

"Well...good luck." The words were spoken sincerely, if not with a great deal of enthusiasm.

"Thank you."

"Give me a call when you get back, will you? You can tell me all about it."

"I'll do that."

Lydia hung up with the hollow feeling that she had disappointed Scott. She rubbed her fingertips over her forehead, reminding herself that she had known better all along than to let herself get involved this way.

She was packing for her trip when Larissa called. "Don't forget it might get chilly up there. Pack some warm clothes."

Lydia smiled wryly, folding a sweater as she held the phone on her shoulder. "Yes, ma'am."

"Sorry. Didn't mean to sound like the bossy older sister."

"Face it, Larissa, you don't really know how to sound any other way when you talk to me."

"Okay, you're right. So I'll just go ahead and say it. Be careful, Lyddie."

"I will. Thanks for caring."

"How does Scott feel about your leaving for this interview?"

"We haven't had much chance to talk about it. He did wish me luck, though."

"Really? He doesn't mind that you might get the job and move so far away?"

"I've told you, Larissa, Scott and I don't have that kind of relationship. He won't interfere."

"Oh. Well, that's good."

Lydia set her sweater in the suitcase and reached for a pair of slacks. "*Now* what's wrong? First you criticized Scott because you were afraid he would get in my way, and now you sound disapproving that he isn't interfering."

Larissa laughed ruefully. "I know. I just worry about you, Lydia. For so long, you and I believed we didn't need anything in our lives but each other and our careers. But now I have Charlie in my life and I've seen how much more there can be. I love my work, you know that. Just as I know how much you love yours. But when the workday ends, it's awfully nice to have someone to talk to. To laugh with. Your work can't give you that."

"So now you're trying to push me into Scott's arms?" Lydia asked in exasperation, ignoring the slightly empty feeling Larissa's words left inside her. "The lawyer?"

"Never mind." Larissa sighed. "I know I'm not making any sense. I've had a rough day—nothing I've attempted has come out right. And…well, to be honest, the thought of you moving all the way to Michigan makes me sad."

"Larissa, I haven't even been offered a position. I'm only going for an interview."

"I know. And I hope you get the job if it's right for you and it's what you want. They would be very fortunate to have you on their team. I'm proud of you, Lyddie, and everything you've accomplished on your own during the past few years.''

Touched, Lydia swallowed before answering. ''Thank you. I'm very proud of you, too.''

''I know.'' Larissa sounded as if she was choking back tears. And then she gave a shaky laugh. ''Lord, I must be hormonal. This is turning into a real fem-fest. Have a good trip, Lyddie. Call me when you get back.''

''I will. Love you, sis.''

''Love you, too.''

Lydia was in a melancholy mood as she finished her packing. Neither Scott nor Larissa had made her feel great about this trip even though both had wished her luck.

She had worked too hard for this to let her sister's uncharacteristic clinginess and Scott's unexpected wistfulness hold her back, she reminded herself. After all, both Larissa and Scott had their own lives and could get along perfectly well without her. She had to take care of herself.

"But when the workday ends, it's awfully nice to have someone to talk to."

Larissa's words seemed to echo in Lydia's empty, quiet bedroom while she finished her packing.

Ten minutes after Lydia walked into her apartment upon her return from Michigan, she called Scott. She had intended to wait a while longer, but her willpower lasted only until she'd set down her luggage.

"Are you home?" he asked the moment he heard her voice.

"Just walked in."

"I'll be up in ten minutes."

He was there in five.

Lydia barely had time to open the door before Scott was inside and she was in his arms. She couldn't even greet him; his mouth covered hers before any sound could emerge.

She had expected to end up in the bedroom. They made it as far as the couch. Her clothes were in a pile on the floor before her back even touched the cushions. Scott was really very good at this, she thought, eagerly drawing him down with her.

She'd spent most of the day in an airplane, cruising at thirty thousand feet. Scott took her even higher.

"So," he asked some time later, when they had slowly drifted back down to earth and could form coherent sentences again, "how was your trip?"

She giggled. Then wondered if that sound had actually come from her.

He shifted his weight, tucking her against his side on the narrow couch. "I missed you."

She ran her hand across his damp skin, feeling his heart still racing in his chest. "I can tell."

Catching her hand, he raised it to his lips. "How *was* your trip?" he asked against her knuckles.

"Long. Tiring. But interesting, I suppose."

"Did they offer you the job?" His voice was a bit too casual to match the expression in his eyes.

"No. They have several people left to interview before they make a decision."

"Do you have any other interviews lined up?"

"A few. I'm flying to Florida Thursday for an interview there."

"No chance you'll end up staying here in Dallas?"

"I didn't say that. There's a chance I'll have an offer here to match any others I might get."

Looking thoughtful, he nodded.

Suddenly uncomfortable with their position, Lydia sat up and reached for her clothes. "I haven't eaten since breakfast," she said. "I'm starving."

He glanced at his watch—the only item he was wearing at the moment, she couldn't help noticing. "It's almost seven. No wonder you're hungry."

While Scott dressed, Lydia wandered into the kitchen to see what she had to eat. She found a package of pasta and some bottled pesto sauce, ingredients she always kept on hand for a quick meal. From the freezer, she unearthed a package of crusty wheat rolls; she put several in the oven to brown while the pasta cooked. Though she hadn't actually asked him, she assumed Scott would stay for dinner.

He kissed the back of her neck when he rejoined her. "Smells good."

"It isn't fancy, but it's filling."

"Oh, yeah, the food." He nuzzled the spot behind her ear. "That smells good, too."

She smiled and stepped aside to stir the sauce. "You are so full of blarney."

Chuckling, he leaned against a counter. "Is there anything I can do to help?"

"Make yourself a drink and have a seat. It'll only take a few minutes."

He rummaged in the refrigerator and pulled out a bottle of wine. "Shall I open this?"

"If you like. It should go well with our meal."

"Wineglasses?"

"First cabinet to the right of the refrigerator."

He found the wineglasses and her other

dishes. By the time the meal was ready, he had the table set. Both hungry, they ate in silence for a few minutes. Scott spoke first. "This is good."

"I always like pasta—but you should know that by now." She thought of the times they had eaten at Vittorio's.

"I'm getting to know quite a few things about you."

There shouldn't have been anything in that simple statement to make her blush—but she did, anyway. She looked quickly down at her plate to hide the inappropriate response.

"You said you'll be in Florida next weekend?"

"Thursday and Friday."

"So you'll be back in town by Sunday?"

"Yes. Why?"

"There's a party Sunday afternoon. I'd like for you to go with me if you're free."

"Is your sister still trying to find a date for you?"

The look he gave her chided her for the question even though she'd asked jokingly.

"I'm asking because I want you with me. There's no other reason now."

"Sorry. What's the purpose of this party?"

His eyebrows rose. "Must a party have a purpose?"

"They generally do."

He shrugged, looking suddenly self-conscious. "It's my birthday, actually. Heather's, too, of course. Shane and Kelly invited the gang to the ranch to mark the occasion."

"Your birthday is next Sunday?"

"Yes. Will you come?"

"Of course. If you don't think my presence will ruin your sister's enjoyment of the day."

"Don't be ridiculous. Heather will be happy to see you. I wish you'd get over this notion that she doesn't like you."

Lydia wrinkled her nose. "I'll take your word for it."

"You said you wanted to see the ranch in daylight. The party starts at two."

"Will there be many guests?"

"Just the usual group. Heather and Steve, of

course. Michael and Judy. You might even have a chance to meet Shane's parents, Jared and Cassie, and his sister, Molly. You'll like them—they're a great family."

She swallowed another bite of her pasta. "You didn't mention Cameron. I assume he'll be there, too?"

"Yes, I'm sure he will. Any particular reason you asked?" he inquired mildly.

"No. Just curious."

He narrowed his eyes at her.

She smiled and dipped her fork into her food again. "It's nice of your friends to help you and Heather celebrate your birthday."

"It was Shane's idea. He said he didn't want our big three-oh to slip by without a shindig."

Lydia's fork clattered against her plate. "You'll be thirty?"

He looked surprised by her reaction. "Yes. Did you think I was older? Younger?"

"Older," she muttered.

"Oh. Does it matter?"

She bit her lip and shrugged, then said ruefully, "I suppose not. It's just that I'm not used to dating younger men."

He started to smile again, his green eyes glinting. "How *much* younger?"

She should have known better than to tease him even a little about Cameron. Scott always found a way to get his own back. She sighed. "I turned thirty-one last December."

"Sixteen months. That's not so very much. Um…would you like me to cut your pasta for you?"

Very calmly, she picked up an extra dinner roll and threw it at him. It hit him squarely in the center of his forehead. Scott laughed.

A moment later, Lydia joined in.

Lydia and Scott spent the rest of the weekend together, turning on their answering machines and hiding in her apartment Saturday night and all day Sunday. She neglected several things she really should have done during those hours and she suspected that Scott did the same, but she couldn't regret it.

It was magical.

She arrived at her office Monday morning in a very good mood, feeling like a woman who was involved in an intense, heart-stopping, teeth-rattling affair with a totally amazing man. It was so unlike her—so far from her usual casual routines—but it felt wonderful.

Everyone should have the opportunity to feel this way at least once. As for how she would feel when it ended—well, there was no need to spoil her good mood by dwelling on the future.

When a delivery of crimson roses arrived at her office that afternoon, she could only shake her head in exasperation. She was a bit surprised to find that Scott had broken his usual pattern and enclosed a card this time. Still no signature—only a brief message: *I can't stop thinking about you.*

How sweet, she thought, touching a fingertip to one velvety petal. She didn't know why it always surprised her so much when he sent her roses. She should be used to it by now—but it always caught her off guard. For some reason, the deliberately anonymous gesture just didn't seem like Scott—which only illustrated how much she had yet to learn about him.

Because they wouldn't be seeing each other that evening, she picked up the phone and dialed his office number, taking a chance on catching him. She was pleased to do so.

"Hi, beautiful. You caught me just before I have to leave for court."

A ripple of pleasure went through her in response to his deep voice. Savoring the feeling, she replied, "I won't keep you. I only wanted to thank you."

"You're welcome. Um...what did I do?"

She wrinkled her nose, thinking that Scott always found time to tease. "You sent roses—again. And it was very nice of you."

"*I* sent roses?"

Her eyebrows shot up. "Didn't you?"

She heard him clear his throat. "As much as I would like to take the credit, I'm afraid I can't. The last time I gave you roses was when you had pizza with me, right after I was sick.

I assume those aren't the ones you called me about."

Her gaze turned slowly to the deep red blooms, seeing them now in an all-new light. "But you sent the others, right?"

"I gave you some on our first date, on Valentine's Day," he answered uncertainly.

"You didn't have *any* roses delivered to my office?"

"I'm afraid not. What's going on, Lydia?"

She sank heavily back into her chair. "I've had three deliveries of roses here during the past couple of months. None of them were signed. I just assumed..."

"You assumed I sent them."

"Yes." She was a little embarrassed now that she'd taken so much for granted.

"I wish I had. You say they weren't signed? No messages?"

"Nothing at all on the first two deliveries. There, um, was a brief message with the arrangement today. But it still isn't signed."

"What does it say?"

"Well..."

"Lydia, what does it say?"

Her cheeks burning, she read him the message.

There was a pause, and when he spoke again, his voice was very serious. "Do you know who could be sending them?"

"I haven't a clue. That's why I thought it must be you."

"When did you get the first ones?"

She thought back. "The Monday after Larissa's party."

"And the next time?"

"Two weeks, maybe ten days later. I don't remember exactly. Before you were ill."

"So that's why you acted so oddly when I gave you the flowers when we shared the pizza. I couldn't understand why you acted like I had given you so many when, as far as I knew, it was only the second time."

"I hardly even remember the last time anyone gave me roses before you," she admitted frankly. "That's why I never imagined I was getting them from two different people."

"And you don't even have a clue who the other person could be?"

"I really don't," she answered. "The only men I've even spent time with lately are you, and that one meal with Cameron—"

"I doubt that it was Cameron. It's just not his style."

"I never thought so, either. Other than that, there was just that one evening with Charlie's friend, Gary Dunston."

"The bookstore guy."

"Yes."

"He was a little strange, Lydia. You have to admit that."

"Yes, I know. That's why I told him there was no reason for him to ask me out again. I tried to be polite, but I made it clear I'm not interested in dating him."

"He could be trying to change your mind."

"With anonymous deliveries? It doesn't seem likely." But who else could it be? She shook her head in frustration, thinking that this was all very strange—and a little spooky.

"What's the name of the florist?"

She read him the name from the delivery card. ''Why?''

''I'll ask around. I don't much like this—for several reasons,'' he confessed wryly. ''Be careful, okay, Lydia? It's probably nothing to worry about, but still, keep an eye out.''

''I doubt that it's a crazy stalker, Scott. There's no need to overreact.''

Her downplaying of the anonymous deliveries didn't seem to reassure him. ''Is there anyone in any of your classes who's been trying particularly hard to get your attention? Hanging out in your office, maybe, or lingering too long after class?''

She thought about it, then shook her head. ''No, not that I can think of. I have a good relationship with several of my students, but nothing out of the ordinary.''

''Be thinking about it. And maybe you should ask your sister a few more questions about Gary.''

''I will. You'd better get to court, Scott. You don't want to be late. Don't worry about this, okay? There's sure to be a perfectly harmless explanation."

"You're probably right." She wished he sounded more convinced.

Chapter Thirteen

When Lydia's doorbell rang that evening, she assumed she would find Scott standing on the other side of the door. He'd told her he had a meeting that would last very late, which was why she hadn't expected to see him. Had her call about the roses made him so uneasy that he'd ducked out of his meeting early?

If so, she was going to have to talk to him. She had told him earlier that there was no need to make too much of this, even if it was a little bizarre. She didn't want to interfere with his work—hadn't that been the very foundation of their relationship?

But when she looked through the peephole, it wasn't Scott's face she saw. Acting more on impulse than caution, she opened the door. "Gary. What are you doing here?"

The perpetually diffident bookstore owner gave her a nervous smile. "I brought you a present," he said, holding out a wrapped package. "It's a new book. It's by a reputable scientist in your field, one you'll agree with more than the author you met when you visited my bookstore, I think."

"That was very thoughtful of you, Gary, but certainly not necessary."

"I wanted to do it," he said earnestly. "I'd still like to make it up to you that you were so uncomfortable in my establishment."

Blocking the doorway with her body, she shook her head, making no effort to reach out for the gift he'd brought her. "Please don't give it another thought."

"I can't seem to help it. Maybe if things had gone better that evening, you would have given me another chance to see you, to get to know each other better."

She almost groaned. ''Really, Gary, that had nothing to do with it. I'm sure you're a very nice man, but I'm afraid I'm just not—''

Gary broke in with a renewed intensity. ''Larissa thinks you and I would be good together. She told me so before she introduced us at her party. As soon as I saw you, I knew she was right. I've admired Larissa since Charlie first introduced me to her, after he and I met and became friends at my store. I've always regretted that he met her first, actually. And then, when I heard she had a sister...''

Lydia almost groaned. This guy was even stranger than she'd first thought. ''Have you been sending roses to my office, Gary?'' she asked although she already knew the answer.

His face brightened. ''Yes. You knew they were from me, didn't you? Larissa mentioned that roses were your favorite flower. Did you like them?''

''I'm going to have to be blunt with you, Gary. I'd rather you didn't send me any more flowers, or call or come by again. There's really no reason to do so. I'm simply not interested in going out with you. I'm sorry if that hurts you, but—''

Perhaps she had allowed his generally meek and harmless appearance to mislead her. It had never seriously entered her mind that he could be a real threat to her.

She was, apparently, more naive than she'd realized. Moving more forcefully than she ever could have expected, Gary shoved against the door, causing Lydia to stumble out of the doorway. He was inside before she could stop him. She heard the door close hard and felt apprehension grip her for the first time since he had rung her doorbell.

She made a quick move toward the door. He moved in front of it, blocking her, his expression beseeching. ''If you'll only listen to me, I'm sure you'll understand that you've misjudged me,'' he said, his voice still unexpectedly soft. ''You haven't really given us a chance.''

On the rare occasions when she had to face angry and defiant students—only a time or two when she'd refused to give passing grades for 'ailing work—she'd found the best course of ıction was to stand firm and show no uncer-ainty. Drawing on that experience, she kept ıer voice steady and deliberately professorial vhen she spoke. ''You aren't helping your :ase with this behavior, Gary. Please leave ıow.''

He didn't seem to be in the least affected by ıer authoritative tone. ''Not until you hear me ›ut.''

''Must I call the police and have you es-:orted from my home?''

His face flushed, making him look even nore agitated. ''I'd really rather you didn't.''

Maybe she was handling this the wrong vay. Gary wasn't a frustrated student, but a 'ejected suitor. Perhaps he would respond bet-er to compassion. ''You have to understand hat it isn't personal,'' she said, attempting a ;mall smile. ''I think you're very nice. But I'm nvolved with someone else.''

''That lawyer?''

She nodded. ''Yes. Scott Pearson. You met ıim at Larissa's party. He's a very special man in my life—and I'm expecting him any minute actually, so—''

''He'll hurt you. Larissa said so.''

''She was wrong. She didn't know him wel then and thought I was still available to mee other people. But she knows now that Scot and I are together and she's accepted it very well. She likes Scott—she even sold him one of her paintings.''

Stubbornly, Gary shook his head. ''I don' like him. He's a shark. Men like that take wha they want and move on. They can't be trusted.''

''You really don't know him. Scott's no like that.''

''The lawyer wants you because you're beautiful, but you need someone who truly ap preciates you. Your mind, your spirit, you soul...''

Lydia blinked. This was definitely getting weird. Even his implication that she was the kind of woman a man would pursue just be cause she looked good on his arm was crazy She wasn't that type.

Gary took a step toward her. "He isn't right for you, Lydia. You should trust your sister on this. Trust *me.*"

"I believe it's up to me to decide whether he's right for me or not."

"We're only trying to protect you. We want to keep you from being hurt."

"I appreciate your concern," she lied, taking a step backward toward the telephone. "But it really isn't necessary."

Still moving toward her, he went on as if he hadn't heard. "I understand why you're attracted to him. Men like him are always surrounded by women who are susceptible to their looks and their charm and their well-practiced words. Do you know how much experience it must have taken for him to become so good at seduction, Lydia? How many women he must have used and discarded along the way?"

Because similar thoughts had crossed her mind a time or two and because she hated hearing them echoed by Gary, Lydia scowled. "I promise I'll think about your warning," she assured him, trying to stay calm. ''Now please go, Gary. You're making me uncomfortable.''

''I don't want to make you uncomfortable. I told you—I want to talk to you. To protect you.''

The only person she needed protection from right now was standing three feet away from her. She wondered if she could dial 9-1-1 before he could get the phone away from her. Her heart was beating so hard she thought he could probably hear it. She knew it was almost deafening her. ''Gary, I—''

The doorbell chimed, cutting through her words. She looked quickly toward the door thinking she'd never heard a more welcome sound.

Gary sighed heavily. ''That's probably the lawyer.''

''Yes, I'm sure it is. Um—may I open the door?'' she asked warily, uncertain of what he might do if she tried to move too quickly.

He looked first surprised, then saddened by her question. ''You really don't understand me, do you, Lydia? I'm no threat to you. I only wanted to talk."

"The way you burst in here—"

"I didn't mean to frighten you. I wanted you to listen to me." He shook his head, suddenly morose again. "I'm not very good with women. Not like him."

He could say that again.

The doorbell rang again, followed by a quick rap on the door and Scott's muffled voice. "Lydia? It's Scott."

"You'd better let him in," Gary suggested glumly.

She all but threw open the door. "Scott," she murmured in relief, reaching out to draw him in, "I'm glad you're here."

He spotted Gary immediately. Tensing, he pulled Lydia close to his side and narrowed his eyes at the other man. "What the hell are you doing here?" His voice was very soft.

"I brought Lydia a gift from my store." Gary indicated the package in his hands as he sidled toward the door. "I was just leaving."

"Damn straight you are. Has he been bothering you, Lydia?"

"He…um…wanted to talk. I heard what he had to say and asked him to leave."

Scott nodded without ever taking his eyes off Gary. "Is there any reason for him to ever return?"

"No. We've said all we need to say."

"You heard her, Dunston. I don't want to see you here again. Lydia and I are together, and I don't appreciate other men bringing her presents. So take your gift with you when you go."

His head bobbing, Gary stepped through the open doorway. "I'm sorry if I disturbed you, Lydia. But I do hope you'll think about what I said."

She didn't want to give him the encouragement of a response. She simply stood close by Scott's side and watched Gary leave. He closed the door behind him.

Scott turned immediately to Lydia. "Are you all right? You're pale."

“He unnerved me,” she admitted. “He’s a very strange man, Scott.”

“Why did you invite him in? I told you—”

“I didn’t exactly invite him in. He sort of pushed past me after I asked him to leave.”

“He forced his way in?” Scott’s face darkened. He seemed poised to move toward the door. “Why, that—”

Lydia put a hand on his arm to deter him. “Just let him go, Scott. Yes, he frightened me a little, but I’m not sure he intended to. He’s just…weird. And intense.”

“I don’t trust him.”

Slowly beginning to relax now that the incident seemed to be over, Lydia managed a weak smile. “That’s what he said about you.”

“If he comes near you again, I’ll break his face.”

She sighed and shook her head. “Cool the testosterone, pal,” she murmured, pushing a hand through her hair. “You’re a lawyer. You know you can’t go around breaking faces.”

“Okay. But I can help you slap a restraining order on him.”

"That sounds like a much more practical course of action, if necessary." She let her hand fall to her side. "I think I'll make some tea. Do you want some?"

He was still almost quivering with the desire to take action. He forced his angry gaze away from the door, searching Lydia's face instead. "You're sure you're all right?"

"I'm fine. Just…shaken," she admitted.

He reached out to pull her into his arms, giving her a warm, bracing hug. "I'm sorry."

Clinging to him, she buried her face in his shoulder. "I'm just glad you're here," she murmured, her voice muffled. "What happened to your meeting?"

"I left early. Ever since I talked to you this afternoon, I've been uneasy. I wanted to check and make sure you were okay."

"I'm sorry I interfered with your work, but I'm very glad you came when you did. Maybe Gary would have left without causing any further trouble, but I'm glad I didn't have to put it to the test."

He buried his hand in her hair and lifted her

face to his. ‘‘So am I. If that guy wants to bother you again, he’s going to have to go through me.’’

He lowered his mouth to hers before she could chide him again for his macho attitude. Giving up any last attempt to appear unfazed by the incident, she wrapped her arms around his neck and burrowed into his kiss.

His hands were warm against her back, offering comfort. Tenderness. Friendship.

And then the embrace changed. The kiss deepened. And Lydia was reminded that this man was more than her friend. He was her lover.

He slid his hands down her back to her hips, pulling her more snugly against him. He wanted something, she realized with a faint smile, but it wasn’t tea. Testosterone was still pumping—and she thought she could put it to better use than breaking Gary’s face.

‘‘Since you missed your meeting, you probably have a couple of free hours,’’ she murmured, keeping one arm looped around his neck as she lifted her free hand to his cheek.

"A couple," he agreed, the smile slowly returning to his eyes.

She traced his lower lip with the tip of one finger. "Whatever shall we do to fill them up?"

"We could always sip our tea very slowly."

Pressing a kiss at the corner of his mouth, she chuckled. "Any other suggestions?"

"We could do your laundry."

"All done." She caught his lower lip lightly between her teeth, then released it.

She was pleased to note that his eyes were starting to glaze. "We could always rotate your mattress," he murmured.

Her smile deepened. "That has potential."

He stepped back and held out his hand to her. "Lead the way."

She placed her hand in his, putting the earlier unpleasantness out of her mind. Scott was here now, and she didn't want to waste one precious moment with him.

* * *

"I just want to say again how sorry I am. If I'd had any idea that Gary would act that way—"

"Larissa, it's okay. I've told you—I don't blame you. But I do reserve the right to remind you of this whenever you get the urge to arrange my life for me in the future."

Lydia was packing again, preparing for her trip to Florida, her telephone balanced on her shoulder. Larissa had probably apologized two dozen times during the past few days, taking full, but unjustified, blame for Gary's behavior Monday evening.

"Charlie had a long talk with Gary yesterday," she added. "He's really not dangerous, Lyddie. He's just...well, weird, as you tried to tell me. He promised he would leave you alone from now on. I, um, think Scott rather frightened him Monday."

Remembering how threatening Scott had looked when he faced Gary in her living room, Lydia wasn't surprised. There had been no doubt in her mind who was the most dangerous of the two men. She'd been very glad Scott had been on *her* side. "Good. I hope he was frightened enough to stay *far* away."

"He told Charlie that you are obviously very much in love with Scott."

Lydia nearly dropped the phone. Quickly regaining her composure, she spoke coolly. "Yes, well, we've just agreed that Gary's a bit delusional."

"You're sure he's not right about this one fact?"

"How many times must I tell you, Scott and I—"

"—don't have that kind of relationship," Larissa finished for her. "So you keep saying."

"Only because it's true. We're very good friends and I hope we can remain so even after the affair ends." Though she couldn't imagine being in the same room with Scott without wanting him, she added silently. Or seeing him with someone else without wanting to cry. All in all, it was probably better that she was moving away.

"Whatever you say, sis. I'm staying out of

it. You definitely don't need me complicating your life again anytime soon.''

''Now don't start apologizing again,'' Lydia warned, hoping Larissa *would* butt out, at least for a little while.

At the time they'd agreed upon, Lydia rang Scott's doorbell Sunday afternoon. He opened it almost immediately.

''Happy birthday,'' she greeted him with a smile.

He kissed her warmly. ''Thank you.''

She had dressed for a casual afternoon at the ranch in a denim vest with a T-shirt and jeans. She didn't own boots, so she wore loafers instead.

''You look great,'' Scott said, ushering her inside and closing the door behind her.

It went without saying that he did, too. He wore his jeans, boots and denim shirt as gracefully as his tailored business suits, looking good enough to make her mouth water. Dragging her gaze away from him, she dug in the macramé bag she'd brought with her and pulled out a small wrapped package. ‘‘I wanted to give you your gift before we leave.’’

He accepted it from her even as he said, ‘‘You didn’t have to get me a present.’’

‘‘I know. I wanted to.’’

While she watched, oddly nervous, he tore away the paper. A moment later, he lifted his eyes to her, looking delighted. ‘‘An old Duofold. Lydia, this is wonderful. I don’t have one quite like this.’’

‘‘It’s a 1927 Duofold Junior,’’ she recited, glancing at the old orange pen she’d found for him. ‘‘Medium nib, in fine to excellent condition. I found it at an antique store in Florida.’’ She’d spent more on it than she probably should have since she knew nothing about the value of collectible pens, but the dealer had seemed knowledgeable and trustworthy, so she had gone with her instincts. She’d wanted to buy Scott something she thought he would genuinely like.

He reached out to snag a hand at the back of her neck and pull her toward him for a long, thorough kiss. ''It's great, sweetheart. You shouldn't have—but thank you.''

And then he kissed her again until both of them almost forgot everything but each other. Lydia finally drew back when his hand found its way beneath her T-shirt.

''We don't have time for that,'' she chided, straightening her clothes. ''We have a birthday party to go to.''

He reached for her again. ''Maybe we'll be a little late.''

''And have your sister speculating about what kept us? No, thank you.''

Muttering about her ''obsession'' with his sister, Scott carefully added the new pen to his collection case, then grudgingly left with her for the party.

They were well underway to the ranch when Lydia decided the time was right to share some news with him. She didn't quite know how to phrase it, especially since she still didn't know exactly how she felt about the development herself. But she needed to tell him. ''I got a call just before I came down to your apartment.''

Looking very relaxed as he drove, Scott slanted an encouraging smile at her. ''Larissa?''

''No. It was a colleague from Florida, a woman I met in graduate school.''

''Did you have a chance to visit with her while you were there?''

''Yes. We had lunch.''

''Was there something she forgot to tell you?''

''Something she didn't yet know. She found out through the grapevine that I'm going to be offered the position there. A full professorship with extensive research opportunities. It's quite an exciting offer.''

She was aware that she didn't sound overly excited. Nor did Scott when he responded. ''That's...great news, Lydia. Congratulations.''

''It's not official yet. Beverly wasn't even supposed to call me, but she couldn't wait.''

"You'll accept the offer, of course." It wasn't a question.

She looked out the passenger window. "I'd be foolish not to. It really is a wonderful opportunity. Exactly what I've been working toward for a long time."

"Then you should be very proud."

"Yes." She laced her fingers in her lap.

"How will your sister feel about your moving so far away?"

"I won't know until I tell her. But she's always fully supported me in my career."

"I'm sure she'll be happy for you. But I know she'll miss having you so close by."

"Yes. I'll miss her, too."

They rode in silence for a while, Lydia continuing to watch the passing scenery through her window. Maybe she was feeling so numb about the news because it had been so long coming, she thought. She'd worked toward this goal for so many years. Now that she'd achieved it, she could hardly process the changes about to take place in her life.

She would be leaving so much behind here

in Dallas. Her sister. Her friends from work. Scott.

It wasn't going to be easy saying goodbye to any of them. But she suspected that saying goodbye to Scott would prove to be the hardest task of all.

It was much later that afternoon when Heather cornered Scott under a shade tree in Shane's backyard while everyone else was involved in a rowdy game of horseshoes nearby. "Having a nice birthday?"

Because he didn't want to spoil hers, he smiled and answered, "Great. How about you?"

"I've never been happier," she said simply, looking at her fiancé, who was chatting with Michael Chang as they watched the game.

"That's nice to hear." He looped an arm around her shoulders and gave her a hug.

She slipped an arm around his waist, looking up at him searchingly. "You seem a little distracted today. Is something bothering you?"

He looked at Lydia, who was being taught

how to properly throw a horseshoe by Cameron—who, Scott thought with a frown, was standing a bit closer to her than absolutely necessary. "No, I'm fine."

Following the direction of his gaze, Heather said, "It was nice of Lydia to give me the pretty wooden music box."

"Yes. She's like that." It still warmed him to think of the pen she'd given him, a gift that signified both thought and effort, something she knew he would like.

"I suppose it's possible that I've misjudged her. She was so good to you while you were sick. I wouldn't have expected her to take that much time away from her work."

The mention of Lydia's work made Scott's stomach tighten. He was still reeling from her announcement that she would soon be moving to Florida. He'd known she was looking for a position, of course, and that there was a good chance she would find one in another state. But to hear her actually say the words, to know it was now only a matter of time…he couldn't even think about it without a sharp pang somewhere in the vicinity of his heart.

"I still think she's very reserved. A little hard to read sometimes," Heather added. "But I suppose she's nice. And you're obviously crazy about her."

He frowned. "What makes you say that?"

She laughed softly. "Are you kidding? You've hardly taken your eyes off her all day."

He grimaced. Heather had no idea why he was reluctant to let Lydia out of his sight today. And he saw no need to tell her yet.

He wasn't really ready to hear himself say out loud that Lydia was leaving. Once again, he'd fallen for a woman whose career was coming between them. The very things that drew him to her—her intelligence, her competence, her drive and ambition—were now taking her away.

He would miss her, he thought, watching pleasure light her face when her horseshoe landed very close to the stake.

"Scott?" Heather had turned to face him

now, her expression concerned. ''Something *is* wrong, isn't it? Darn it, I was right after all. She's making you unhappy. If you would only listen to me—''

Before she could get all wound up again, Scott pasted on a grin—hoping it looked reasonably genuine—and reached out to ruffle his sister's hair. ''Give it a rest, Heather. I am not unhappy. I'm having a great time. But I'm hungry. Let's go see if there are any more of those chocolate things Kelly made or if those greedy pals of ours have gobbled them down already.''

He knew she wasn't satisfied, but he had no intention of discussing it any further with her. Whatever happened now, it was strictly between him and Lydia.

Chapter Fourteen

It really was strange, Lydia thought several weeks later, how fast time could speed by. The days following the birthday party simply weren't long enough for her to accomplish everything she needed and wanted to do.

The seasons changed almost without her noticing. It seemed that overnight the trees were in full foliage and the days turned suffocatingly warm. By mid-June, arrangements were under way for her move to Florida, and she had finally added the letters Ph.D. after her name. Larissa, Charlie and Scott had been in the audience to applaud her when she was awarded the degree a couple of weeks earlier.

During those weeks, she and Scott spent as much time together as possible—which wasn't often since they were both so busy. They didn't talk much about her upcoming move. Lydia didn't know exactly how Scott felt about her leaving.

She only knew it was ripping her heart out to leave him.

She'd spent hours debating her decision with herself. She liked living in Dallas, loved being close to Larissa and Scott. But she also loved her work, and the position in Florida was exactly what she had hoped to find. She couldn't justify turning it down because she was involved with a man who had made no commitment to her. Even if he did express an interest in a long-term relationship, could she really turn her back on this opportunity without regrets?

She wasn't so sure she could.

To her relief, there were no more deliveries of roses and no more phone calls from Gary.

On the whole, Lydia thought, she should have been happy with the way her life was going. And yet she had never felt more conflicted.

"You're miserable," Larissa said flatly, having met Lydia for a late lunch one weekday afternoon.

"Now don't start again," Lydia said wearily. "I'm not miserable. I'm just a little tired. I've been so busy lately trying to get ready for this big move."

"I'd like to believe it's the thought of leaving me that's making you so unhappy—but I know the truth. You're grieving about leaving Scott, aren't you?"

"I'll miss him," Lydia acknowledged quietly. "But I've known all along this would happen. It isn't as if I've been deluding myself."

"You really do love him, don't you?" Larissa asked gently.

"I..." Lydia swallowed, unable to lie. "Yes. But that's something I'll learn to live with."

"I can't believe I'm even going to ask

this—but have you thought about staying in Dallas? Settling for a somewhat lesser position so you can be with Scott?''

''I've thought about it. I even tried very hard to talk myself into it. But I can't. It wouldn't be fair to Scott or to me if I walked away from everything I've worked for just to be with him. That's an emotional burden he shouldn't have to shoulder.

''You know how much Mother regretted her decision to turn her back on her dreams for our father's sake. Maybe he didn't deserve her sacrifice—or maybe she expected too much in return. But in the end, they were both unhappy and Mother never got over it. I wouldn't want to ever end up in that position. I would be willing to make compromises for a relationship—big compromises, perhaps. But a sacrifice of this magnitude? I don't know if I have that much courage.''

She toyed with the nearly untouched food on her plate. ''This is all hypothetical anyway. Scott has never asked me to stay.''

''And if he did? If he told you he loves you

and he doesn't want you to go? What would you say then?''

''I don't know,'' Lydia murmured. ''I think I would still make the same choice—but I don't really know if I could still be so strong. I suppose it's best that he hasn't asked.''

Someone stopped beside the table, throwing a shadow on Lydia's plate. She glanced up automatically, then almost winced when she recognized the woman standing there.

''Heather,'' she said, wondering how much, if anything, Scott's sister had overheard, ''how are you?''

''Fine, thank you. My wedding consultant and I are having lunch across the room, and when I saw you, I wanted to say hello.''

Lydia motioned toward Larissa. ''This is my sister, Larissa. Larissa, this is Scott's sister, Heather Pearson.''

''Actually,'' Heather said, shaking Larissa's hand, ''we've met very briefly before. It was at the Valentine's Day charity auction. I bought one of your paintings. It's hanging in my new living room right now—I love it.''

Gracious as always to anyone who complimented her work, Larissa smiled. "Yes, I remember meeting you. How nice to see you again."

"Heather's going to be married soon," Lydia said, trying to make conversation.

"One more week," Heather agreed brightly. "And a zillion things to do in the meantime."

"How exciting for you," Larissa said.

"Yes. You *are* coming, aren't you, Lydia?"

"Yes, of course. I'm looking forward to it." Heather had sent Lydia a lovely invitation, and Scott had already said he wanted her to go with him.

"Great. I better get back to my planning. It was nice to see you again, Larissa. And, Lydia, we'll be seeing each other soon."

Lydia watched Heather bustle away, then faced her sister again and groaned. "I hope she didn't overhear what we were saying."

Larissa looked after Scott's sister thoughtfully. "I wonder..."

Scott and Heather stood in the vestibule of the church where Heather and Steve would be married the next day, waiting for their cue to make a practice walk down the aisle.

"Hang on a minute," Avis, the briskly efficient wedding consultant told them. "I need to make some changes in there. I'll let you know when I want you to come in."

Scott sighed. "Just how long is this rehearsal going to take, Heather? We've already been through it twice."

"Now, Scott, I'm only going to be married once. I want it to be perfect."

Guiltily reining in his impatience, Scott forced a smile. "Of course you are. And we'll go through it as many times as you like."

She pouted. "You only want to hurry so you can get back to Lydia."

"Heather, I said I'm willing to go through it again. Lydia has nothing to do with this."

She didn't seem appeased. "The most important time in my life, and all you can think about is your big-shot doctor girlfriend."

He nearly sighed. After seeming for a while to have accepted Lydia's presence in Scott's life, Heather had undergone a change during the past week. She'd been very critical of Lydia, missing few opportunities to get in a dig at her. He didn't know what had set her off, but he'd tried to be patient, blaming it on her nervousness and anxiety about the upcoming wedding. But it was getting more difficult to hold his tongue. "I'd rather not talk about Lydia. We have other things to concentrate on now."

Heather ignored the broad hint. "When is she moving?"

"Next month. Now, do we start out on our left foot or our right when we hear the music?" he asked, trying to distract her.

"Left. When next month?"

"Early." Two weeks, he thought. Lydia would be leaving his life in two short weeks. Already most of her belongings were packed in boxes and suitcases. He had hardly been able to step into her apartment lately, preferring instead to spend time with her at his place where there were fewer reminders of her imminent departure.

"Good."

Scott scowled. "You needn't sound so pleased about it. Damn it, Heather, I'm going to miss her."

She rolled her eyes. "Please don't tell me you've asked her to stay."

"Of course not. I wouldn't do that."

"Hey, you're the one who was just whining about how much you're going to miss her."

"I was *not*—" Scott forced himself to stop and lower his voice. "I wasn't whining. I merely stated a fact. And I haven't asked her to stay because that would be unfair to Lydia. An opportunity like this doesn't come along every day. She would be crazy to turn it down, and I would be a jerk to ask her to. You don't just ask someone to walk away from a life's dream, Heather."

"I see." She smoothed the pretty dress she'd worn for the rehearsal. "Well, that's very noble of you, I suppose."

Damn straight it was, Scott thought grimly. Heather had no idea how often he'd had to bite his tongue to keep himself from begging Lydia not to go.

Checking her reflection in a decorative mirror on the wall, Heather said, ‘‘I’m just glad you haven’t come up with a harebrained notion like moving to Florida with her. Your life is here, and I don’t want you to forget that. It’s not as if you’re in love with her or anything. You never have any trouble finding women to spend time with. Maybe once Lydia’s out of the picture, you’ll give my friend Julie a chance. She’s still available, you know. And although she likes her job as a kindergarten teacher, she doesn’t intend to let it keep her from getting married and having a family once she finds the right guy.’’

Only the reappearance of Heather’s wedding consultant kept Scott from strangling his sister. Okay, he thought, so maybe he wouldn’t have actually strangled her. But he might have made her wish he had.

He’d never heard such nonsense in his life—even from Heather. So why did her words keep echoing in his mind as he walked her down the aisle? And why did Heather keep smiling at him so oddly—almost resignedly?

"So how was the rehearsal?" Lydia asked Scott much later that evening, speaking from the hollow of his bare shoulder, where she had burrowed to recover her strength. Still damp and heavy-limbed from lovemaking, they lay in the tangled sheets of her bed.

They had hardly spoken since he arrived. Scott had taken her in his arms the minute she opened the door to him, and they'd ended up in the bedroom only moments later.

"The rehearsal was long," he answered her. "And boring. They made us keep doing the same things over and over."

"That's to make sure you do it right when it counts."

"Yeah, well, we'll see. Steve and I have a bet that the flower girl is going to wimp out when she has to perform in front of an audience. She's cute as a button, but shy."

"I'm sure she'll be adorable. And you and Steve shouldn't be placing bets on possible wedding glitches. Heather would be very put out with you both if she knew.''

He shrugged. ''Steve had better get used to Heather being put out. I know I am.''

''Still, her wedding day is very important. You shouldn't joke about it.''

''I have to admit I find some of this wedding stuff kind of silly. Wouldn't she be just as married without all the fuss and fancy?''

''Of course. But some women like the fuss.''

He toyed with a strand of her hair, twirling it around his finger. ''Heather definitely likes being the center of attention.''

''That doesn't surprise me,'' she said with a chuckle.

Supporting himself on one elbow, he propped his head on his hand, looking down at her. ''I'm glad you'll be with me at the wedding. You can keep me out of trouble.''

''And just how am I supposed to do that?''

''If I get out of line, you can give me that look you do so well. You know, your professor look.''

She laughed. "'I don't know if my 'professor look' would have much effect on you.''

''Surely you know by now that everything you do has an effect on me.''

She might have blushed a little. The room was too shadowy for him to be sure. ''More of your blarney,'' she murmured.

He kissed the tip of her nose. ''Just stating facts.''

''I'm thirsty,'' she said, sitting up and reaching for her robe. ''I need a glass of water. Do you want anything?''

''Actually, I'm thirsty, too.'' He stepped into his slacks and followed her toward the kitchen without bothering with shirt or socks. He stumped his toe hard on a packing box halfway across the living room. Hopping inelegantly, he muttered an obscenity.

Lydia turned in the kitchen doorway. ''Are you okay?''

''Do you have to leave these boxes all over the floor like this? Someone could get hurt.''

He didn't usually speak so crossly to her

She blinked, then said, "I'm sorry. I should have pushed it closer to the wall."

He sighed and shook his head. "No, I'm sorry. I shouldn't have snapped at you that way. It was my fault for not paying attention."

"It's late. You're tired. I understand."

Entering the kitchen, he accepted a glass of water from her. "It isn't just that," he admitted. "I guess I really hate seeing these packing boxes. I don't like the reminder that you'll be leaving so soon."

She sipped her water and looked away from him.

"I'll miss you, Lydia," he said after a moment.

"I'll miss you, too."

He studied her face, trying to read her expression. He couldn't help remembering Heather's criticism that Lydia kept her feelings well hidden so that he would never really be sure how she felt about him.

He knew she had some reservations about her move. Natural doubts about leaving her home, moving away from her sister, starting a new job. And she had said she would miss him. But how did she *really* feel about leaving him?

It hadn't hurt like this when Paula moved away. He and Paula had agreed from the start that they wouldn't always be together—just as he and Lydia had implied. But he'd never been tempted to try to change Paula's mind. He had missed her in some ways—after all, they'd had some great times together—but her absence hadn't left a hole in his life.

Lydia was going to leave a very large hole behind. One he didn't quite know how he was going to fill.

The wedding, for all its ''fuss and fancy'' as Scott had called it, was beautiful. Lydia sat with Michael and Judy Chang during the ceremony while Scott escorted his sister down the aisle and then moved to stand as one of Steve's attendants. She thought the nontraditional arrangement was very sweet, signifying Scott's full approval of this wedding.

A lavish reception followed the ceremony

The band Heather had hired was very good, the caterer excellent, the decorations lovely. If she were the type of woman who dreamed of big, splashy weddings, this was exactly what she would have wanted, Lydia reflected.

Though she had never considered herself overly sentimental, she felt tears mist her eyes when Heather and Steve exchanged their vows. She told herself that it was only happiness for the other couple causing her heart to ache. Certainly not envy.

Scott stayed close to Lydia's side during the reception. Together they mingled with his friends, making conversation, enjoying themselves immensely—though it was obvious Scott wished everyone would quit asking about Lydia's upcoming move. Every time it came up, he found a way to quickly change the subject.

"Are you all packed?" Cameron asked, ignoring Scott's frown.

"Almost," she answered. "I'll be doing a lot of last-minute box stuffing, but I have it pretty much under control."

"I'll miss seeing you at our gatherings."

She smiled at Cameron, whom she now considered a friend. "That's very nice. Thank you."

"You'll be back to visit, won't you?"

"Of course. My sister's here. I hope to be back often to visit her."

"And I hope you'll be able to visit us, as well."

She smiled without answering. She didn't know if she would see Scott's friends again—for that matter, she didn't even know if she would be seeing Scott again. They hadn't discussed staying in contact after she moved. They were both so carefully avoiding talk about the move, she mused ruefully. It was as if they thought that if they ignored it long enough, they wouldn't have to deal with it.

Proving that he was still in no mood to discuss it, Scott took her arm. "Let's go dance."

Accompanying him to the dance floor, she followed his example and pushed the move to the back of her mind. She wanted to enjoy the rest of the day and she couldn't do that if she dwelled on the near future.

Heather cornered Lydia alone not long before the reception ended. "Well?" she asked, beaming happily. "What did you think of my wedding?"

"It was beautiful," Lydia answered sincerely. Then added just as candidly, "And so are you."

Heather's smile deepened as she patted her lace-and-satin gown. "Thank you. I know Scott's been making fun of me for wanting all the pomp and ceremony, but I've dreamed of a wedding like this since I was a girl. And it was everything I'd hoped it would be."

"I'm sure you and Steve will be very happy together."

"I think so, too." Heather's expression suddenly became harder to read. "So you're moving in another couple of weeks?"

Lydia nodded. "I'll be gone before you return from your honeymoon."

Smiling mysteriously, Heather murmured, "I'm sure we'll be seeing each other again. I have an instinct for knowing things like that, you know.''

Lydia found herself at a loss for words. There were times when Scott's sister was a total enigma to her.

''Heather, let's have one more dance before we leave,'' Steve said, approaching the two women with Scott trailing just behind him.

She whirled to her new husband eagerly. ''Of course.'' Glancing over her shoulder at Lydia, she added quietly, ''I've planted the seed for you. We'll just have to wait and see if it took root. But I just want you to know that it wasn't an easy choice for me.''

Lydia had no idea what Heather was talking about. She watched her leave in utter bewilderment.

Scott slid an arm around her waist. ''So what were you and my sister discussing so intently over here?''

''To be honest,'' she said, looking rather blankly up at him, ''I'm not absolutely sure.''

He chuckled wryly. ''Yeah. That sounds

like a typical conversation with my sister. Let's go enjoy this last dance, shall we?"

Last dance. Even those words struck Lydia with a pang. She hid the reaction behind a bright smile. "Yes, let's."

They spent her last night in Dallas in Scott's apartment since Lydia's was empty. They didn't waste much of the night sleeping.

Lydia was making coffee for breakfast when Scott slid his arms around her waist from behind, burying his face in her hair. "What will I do without you?" he murmured.

She swallowed, keeping her eyes on what she was doing. "Make your own coffee?"

"That isn't what I meant, and you know it."

She sighed lightly. "I know."

"Have I mentioned that I really hate it that you're moving away?"

He hadn't, actually. He had merely alluded to it that one night before Heather's wedding.

"I'll miss you, Lydia."

She closed her eyes and leaned back against him. "I'll miss you, too."

Very slowly, he turned her to face him. His hands on her shoulders, he studied her face, which she knew must show the strain of her emotions. "What would you have said," he asked quietly, "if I had asked you not to go?"

"I..." She swallowed, a surge of panic rising to almost strangle her. "I honestly don't know."

His gaze bored into hers, his eyes much more serious than his tone. "Shall I try it and see?"

Her heart jumped straight into her throat, making it even harder to speak. "I really hope you don't," she whispered.

He looked tempted to do so anyway. She didn't know if she was relieved or disappointed when he grimaced and nodded. "You're right, of course. It would be an incredibly selfish move on my part. I want only the best for you, Lydia. And that seems to be in Florida for now."

She swallowed. "I hope you're right."

His smile was strained. "I'm sure it will be everything you hoped it would be."

She bit her lip.

''The coffee's ready,'' Scott said, moving away. ''You take cream, don't you?''

She blinked rapidly to clear a hot film from her eyes. ''Yes. Cream. No sugar.''

Though he'd had little sleep the night before, Scott spent most of that night pacing through his apartment. It seemed so quiet. So empty. Even emptier knowing that there was no one in the apartment upstairs.

He shouldn't have let her go, he thought, thumping his fist against a wall. He should have begged her to stay. Something about the way she'd looked at him with her heart in her eyes just before they parted had told him he might have talked her into staying.

And eventually she would have hated him for it.

He hit the wall again.

I'm just glad you haven't come up with a harebrained notion like moving to Florida with her.

The recurring echo of Heather's words from

the wedding rehearsal caused a by now familiar reaction inside him—pure panic. Leave everything he had here to trail after a woman who had never indicated she even wanted to see him again? He would be insane to do so.

He had to face it. It wasn't meant to be. What he and Lydia shared had been spectacular, but it was over. They were both moving on. They would get past this.

But it hurt, he thought. It hurt very badly.

It's not as if you're in love with her or anything, he could hear Heather saying again.

He muttered a curse and turned away from the wall before he was tempted to hit it hard enough to break his hand.

Chapter Fifteen

Even after living in Florida for six weeks, there were still things Lydia had yet to grow accustomed to. Dallas tended to be casual, but she found Florida even more so. The ready availability of fresh seafood was wonderful, but she still hadn't found a restaurant she liked quite as well as Vittorio's. She could already tell she was going to love her job, but she still had a ways to go before she would feel completely at ease.

She missed Dallas, but she liked her new surroundings and could see herself being content here eventually.

She and Larissa stayed in close contact by telephone. It wasn't as nice as being able to see her whenever she wanted, of course, but she knew they would always be close in spirit no matter how many miles separated them.

She hadn't heard from Scott.

To say that she missed him would have been a massive understatement. Not one hour passed that she didn't think about him, if only in passing. She had left part of her heart in Dallas with him, and the only thing she knew to do was to learn to live without that part of herself.

There were times when she lay awake, missing him so badly her entire body ached. Wondering if she had made a huge mistake by leaving Dallas and everyone she loved there. By leaving Scott.

Maybe she should have stayed. This was, after all, only a job. And as Larissa had once pointed out, a job couldn't keep her company after hours. Couldn't hold her during the long, lonely nights.

Those doubts haunted her in the darkness.

But with the sunrise came the certainty that she had made the right choice. What else could she have done?

It was a Saturday afternoon, and Lydia was stretched out on her couch with a can of diet soda and a fast-paced romantic suspense novel. A selection of soothing New Age music played from her CD player. One of the resolutions she made when she took this drastic step in her life had been to make more time for herself from now on. Time for relaxation. Pleasure. She might even find a hobby eventually.

When the doorbell rang, her first thought was to ignore it. This was her time, she thought. There was no one she wanted to see now.

No one in this particular state anyway.

But even as the thought crossed her mind, she knew she wouldn't be able to ignore the bell. Her natural curiosity wouldn't allow it.

By long-ingrained habit, she checked to see who was on the other side before she opened the door. At first, she couldn't believe her eyes.

Had she fallen asleep on the couch? Was she dreaming? Hallucinating?

Very slowly, she opened the door. "Scott?"

"Hello, Lydia."

It was startling enough to find him there. But equally surprising was what he was wearing. A red-and-white tropical-print shirt. Board shorts. Sandals. She had seen Scott in business wear and Western wear, but this was the first time she'd seen him in surf-bum chic.

"I can't believe you're here," she said dazedly. Why hadn't he called first? What did he want? What were the odds that she could handcuff him to her bed and keep him there forever?

"Well?" He held out his arms as if modeling his outfit for her. "How do I look?"

"You look...different."

He nodded as if satisfied with her answer. "May I come in?"

Still numb, she moved aside.

Scott passed her, studying the bright, airy living room of her town house apartment with interest. "This is very nice. I like all the windows. Great view."

"Thanks." She shut the door, turning to stare at him again. Her heart was beating so fast, so hard, she could hardly speak. For the first time since she left Dallas, she felt whole again.

It terrified her.

"Why are you here?" she asked, almost dreading the answer. If he had come to ask her to return to Dallas with him, she didn't know if she could refuse, no matter how much she liked it here, no matter what she would be giving up for him. Whatever the consequences, she had fallen deeply in love with Scott Pearson and she couldn't keep torturing herself by trying to deny that fact.

He turned away from the big windows to look at her. "I turned thirty recently. But you knew that, didn't you?"

Maybe she *was* dreaming. Nothing seemed to be making sense. "Yes. I was there."

"Which is what made it so special," he said with one of his sexy, single-dimpled smiles.

She almost gulped.

"Anyway, when a man reaches the age of thirty, it seems like he should take stock of his life. Where he's been. Where he's headed. What he wants."

"And?" she whispered, holding herself steady with one hand on the back of a chair.

He answered with another confusing subject change. "I have some good news to share with you. I was offered a full partnership in the law firm yesterday."

She couldn't help remembering the drive to Shane's ranch on Scott's birthday, when she had shared her own career news with him. "Congratulations, Scott. I'm very—"

"I turned it down."

Stunned, she clutched the chair with both hands. She could feel the blood drain from her face. "You did *what?*"

"I turned it down."

"Scott, why? It was your dream."

"No. It was a goal, not a dream. I've only recently realized that there's a difference. Once

I reached that goal, I knew it was time to move on."

Maybe she should try pinching herself. This simply could not be real. "What—what are you going to do?"

He straightened his wildly patterned shirt. "I'm looking for a change of scenery. Texas is great, but it's time for new experiences. I can practice law anywhere, once I've obtained the proper licenses."

"Here?" Her voice was barely audible. "You're moving here?"

He was still smiling, but his eyes were very intense when he looked at her. "Yes. I have a new goal, you see."

"What new goal?"

"Convincing you to marry me. This goal is also a dream, by the way. One I expect to fulfill me for a lifetime."

"I *am* dreaming," she said out loud. There was no way this was really happening.

He chuckled softly. "No. It's real."

"I..." She couldn't for the life of her make her tongue respond to her will.

"My sister says you keep your emotions very well hidden," Scott said, sounding suddenly a bit uncertain. "She says she can never tell exactly what you're thinking or feeling. I've got to admit, I know what she's talking about right now."

It would help, Lydia thought, if *she* knew what she was feeling. Other than terror, of course. Other than a wild, reckless, almost overwhelming urge to throw herself in his arms and hold him forever. "Scott—"

"I know I've got my work cut out for me," he went on doggedly. "We didn't plan on anything like this. You certainly never said you wanted me to join you in your new life here. Maybe, like the woman I knew in law school, you think you need to be on your own to accomplish your goals. But, whatever it requires, however long it takes, I'm going to convince you that this is right, Lydia. That we're perfect together. That we were meant to be together."

"Yes."

"I'm going to show you that I would never stand in your way, that I can be a partner to you in every way. If we choose to have a family, I'll be there to help you with..." He paused, frowning. "What did you just say?"

"Yes." She said it rather more firmly this time.

"Yes, what?" he asked, sounding as if he wasn't entirely sure they were talking about the same thing.

"Yes, I'll marry you."

"Oh." He looked suddenly as stunned as she felt. "But I haven't even asked you yet."

She was now torn between kissing him and punching him. If he was only toying with her... "Well?" she prompted.

Very slowly, his eyes began to lighten as his smile invaded them. "Lydia McKinley, will you do me the great honor of marrying me? In a civil ceremony or a lavish affair with all the trimmings—whatever you want, as long as it's forever."

"Yes," she said again. After all the debate, all the stress, all the worry, it turned out she'd never been more certain of anything in her life.

His grin was full, almost blinding. "That was a lot easier than I expected."

She finally released the chair and stepped toward him. "I'm still not entirely convinced I'm not dreaming."

He moved a step in her direction. "What would it take to convince you?"

"You could pinch me, I suppose."

His grin turned wicked. "Oh, Lydia. I'm going to do a lot more than that."

Finally, she was in his arms and his mouth was on hers. And if she was dreaming, she knew she never wanted to wake up.

Scott spared only a glance at Lydia's new bedroom before he turned to her beside the bed. "Very nice," he said—but he was looking at her, not the decor.

She smiled. "About those clothes..."

He glanced down. "What about them?"

"I'm not sure they're really you."

"Not even the new Florida me?"

Laughing, she shook her head. "I miss my Texan."

He reached out to pull her into his arms. ''I'm real glad to hear that, ma'am,'' he said in an exaggerated drawl.

She tugged his head down to hers. ''Just be quiet and kiss me, will you?''

''With pleasure,'' he murmured, then proceeded to do so until neither of them could tease any longer.

With long, deep, hungry kisses, they attempted to make up for all the lonely days they had spent apart. Their hands raced over each other, eager to compensate for lost time. Clothes flew, landing in multicolored puddles across the sand-colored carpet. The bed rocked when they fell heavily onto it.

Lydia no longer worried that she might be dreaming. No mere dream could make her feel this good. Only Scott could do that.

As if he was afraid he might have forgotten some minor detail, Scott reexplored every inch of her, trailing his lips and fingertips from the hollow of her throat to the swell of her breasts, and then slowly, tantalizingly lower. Along the way, he nipped, nibbled and licked until she was writhing with sensations almost too intense to bear. And when she arched and cried out, he gave her even more.

"I love you," he murmured just before he joined them with one powerful thrust.

She would have repeated the words, but he had completely deprived her of the power of speech. She settled instead for showing him exactly how she felt.

She must have fallen asleep. There were long shadows in the bedroom when she opened her eyes. Needing reassurance again that it hadn't been a dream, she lifted her head and looked at the pillow next to hers. She smiled in relief when she saw Scott lying there awake, one hand behind his head, the other lying on his flat stomach.

"Hi," he said.

"You're really here."

His smile turned tender. "There's nowhere else I'd rather be."

Pulling the sheet snugly beneath her arms, she shifted to prop herself on one elbow, facing him. "You really turned down the partnership? Gave up your job with the firm in Dallas?"

"I really did. So I sure hope you like your job here."

"I do, actually. Very much."

"I'm glad to hear that. It's a beautiful area. I think we'll like living here, don't you?"

"Yes, I think we will." She ran a fingertip down his arm, feeling the muscles beneath his skin. "Have you, um, told your sister?"

"Yes. I called her yesterday. Yours, too, for that matter."

"You called *my* sister?"

"Yes. I suppose I wanted her blessing, too. She said she wondered what was taking me so long to follow you here. And then she wished me luck."

Apparently, Larissa had decided to give her approval to this match even if Scott was still a lawyer. "I have a feeling *your* sister didn't react quite so positively. I'm sure she's still sobbing at the thought of you moving away."

He shook his head against the pillow. "You

continue to underestimate my sister. Heather didn't try to stop me from this move. In fact, she claims full credit for giving me the idea."

She couldn't have heard him correctly. "I beg your pardon?"

"It was something she said during her wedding rehearsal. She pretended to be glad we were going our separate ways, but she said that was only an act. According to her, she was actually encouraging me to come after you."

Lydia was stunned. She remembered that Heather had said something at her wedding about having "planted the seed," but she'd had no idea it was anything like this. "What made her change her mind about me?"

"I'm not sure exactly. She said it was something she overheard that convinced her we were right for each other after all. She said she had an 'instinct' about it," he added wryly.

Lydia laughed. "I can't believe it."

"Hey, that's my sister. I gave up trying to figure her out a long time ago."

"I know she'll miss you terribly."

"As much as Larissa misses you," he

agreed seriously. ‘‘As much as we’ll miss them in return. But our sisters have their own lives. It’s time for us to get on with ours. We’ll visit them often—and we’ll make sure to let them see that we knew what we were doing all along when we ignored their matchmaking to find our own partners.’’

‘‘Has it occurred to you that it’s *because* of our sisters’ matchmaking that we ended up together? So maybe they should get the credit after all.’’

Scott almost shuddered. ‘‘Don’t even think that when you’re around them. If we give them the credit, we’ll never hear the end of it.’’

She smiled and leaned down to kiss him. And then sent a silent thank-you to Larissa and Heather for making this surprise partnership possible.

* * * * *